Willis S Webb

Incidents and Trials in the Life of Rev. Eugenio Kincaid

Willis S Webb

Incidents and Trials in the Life of Rev. Eugenio Kincaid

ISBN/EAN: 9783337193669

Printed in Europe, USA, Canada, Australia, Japan

Cover: Foto ©Andreas Hilbeck / pixelio.de

More available books at **www.hansebooks.com**

Your ever affectionate
Eugenie Kincaid

INCIDENTS AND TRIALS

IN THE LIFE

—OF—

Rev. EUGENIO KINCAID, D.D.

—THE—

"HERO" MISSIONARY TO BURMA.

1830—1865.

—BY—

Rev. WILLIS S. WEBB.

FORT SCOTT, KANSAS:
MONITOR PUBLISHING HOUSE AND BOOK BINDERY.
—1890—

TO HIS

CHILDREN WHO SURVIVE HIM

AND

ITTLE CHURCH WHICH ENJOYED HIS COUNCILS, WHERE HIS
SUN WENT DOWN IN FULL ORBED GLORY,

THIS VOLUME

IS AFFECTIONATELY AND GRATEFULLY INSCRIBED

BY

THE AUTHOR.

INTRODUCTION.

With the view of doing good to the cause of missions and aiding the little church of which Dr. Kincaid died an honored member, in its efforts to erect in Girard, Kansas, "The Kincaid Memorial Church Edifice," I undertook the work of rewriting and setting in order some of the thrilling incidents in the life of one of the greatest missionaries ever sent out by our "American Baptist Missionary Union."

The subject of our sketch entered the field when there were but two churches in Burma. He lived to see Christian homes and churches established in every part of the empire. Some difficulty has been experienced in collecting and setting in order some of the hitherto unwritten incidents; some are written as I remember to have heard him relate them. I do not hope to escape criticism by giving a perfect recital of only the more prominent events in a life and career second only in importance to our First American Baptist Missionary, Dr. Judson; and, in point of endurance, dauntless courage, and unselfish devotion to the Master's work, surpassed by none.

Hoping the book may have such a reading as will revive in some measure the interest kindled in missions by Dr. Kincaid's own recitals and stirring appeals during his visits to America, and that some worthy young man may take up the work laid down by the "Hero," whose labor is ended, and lay himself on the altar of consecrated work for Jesus. With prayer and hope I send it on its mission.

WILLIS S. WEBB.

Girard, Kansas, July, 1890.

CONTENTS.

	PAGE
CHAPTER I.	11
BIRTH—SCHOOLDAYS—BAPTISM.	
CHAPTER II.	24
ELEMENTS AND TRAITS OF CHARACTER.	
CHAPTER III .	35
LONGING FOR A FOREIGN FIELD.	
CHAPTER IV.	43
ENTERING THE FIELD—WIFE'S DEATH.	
CHAPTER V	52
A YEAR IN RANGOON—A SECOND MARRIAGE.	
CHAPTER VI.	60
FROM RANGOON TO AVA.	
CHAPTER VII.	68
OPPOSITION AT THE CAPITAL.	
CHAPTER VIII	78
THE GOSPEL IN AVA.	
CHAPTER IX.	85
SOWING BESIDE FRESH WATERS.	
CHAPTER X	95
CAPTURED BY ROBBERS.	
CHAPTER XI.	105
IN GREATER PERILS.	
CHAPTER XII.	121
THE COUNTRY AND PEOPLE VISITED.	

PAGE.

CHAPTER XIII............   128
REACHING HOME -- REVOLUTION—CHANGE OF FIELD.

CHAPTER XIV.................................   144
A GRACIOUS WORK IN ARRACAN.

CHAPTER XV.............   154
VISIT TO THE MOUNTAIN CHIEF, CHETZA.

CHAPTER XVI.....   166
A VISIT TO AMERICA.

CHAPTER XVII................................   175
BARRIERS BREAKING AWAY.

CHAPTER XVIII..........   191
ENROUTE AGAIN FOR BURMA

CHAPTER XIX......................... 201
RESUMING WORK.

CHAPTER XX.......................... 214
HAVING FAVOR WITH ALL THE PEOPLE.

CHAPTER XXI.. 225
INTERRUPTED BY WAR.

CHAPTER XXII......................... 241
NEGLECTED PROME, A FIELD OF PROMISE.

CHAPTER XXIII..................... 248
IN FAVOR WITH THE KING.

CHAPTER XXIV......................... 257
SERVING THE KING.

CHAPTER XXV...................... 268
LAST YEARS IN BURMA.

CHAPTER XXVI...................... 276
HIS KANSAS HOME.

Incidents and Trials in the Life of
E. KINCAID.

INCIDENTS AND TRIALS IN THE LIFE OF EUGENIO KINCAID

CHAPTER I.

BIRTH—SCHOOL DAYS—BAPTISM.

To Noah Kincaid, a respectable physician, and Lydia Hough Kincaid, his wife, in their home at Weathersfield, Connecticut, January 9th, 1797, was born, the eldest of eight children, Eugenio Kincaid.

His parents were consistent members of the Presbyterian church, and highly esteemed for their good qualities and devotion to the Master's cause. Like others of this good people they wanted their children to receive the rite of baptism, but had neglected the matter until Eugenio was old enough to offer some objections; but, finally, asking "what good will it do?" was told by his father if it did no good it could do no harm, he waived his objections and received the rite of baptism at the age of twelve years after the manner of his people.

So he needed only confirmation to admit him to full membership with the people of his choice.

Nothing very striking in his early life seems worthy of special mention, except his great thirst for knowledge, and the occasional outcroppings of his Scotch grit and determination to obtain the most liberal education possible amid his surroundings.

It was a struggle then, with limited means and few books, to work one's way up to the academy or high school. But urged on by his unfaltering purpose to develop and use whatever powers he possessed or might acquire, every obstacle must be surmounted.

He borrowed and read books and taught school and studied until the time arrived that he was urged to appear before the session for full membership. For this action he could see no good reason, and declined because of some disagreement with the answer to the question in the catechism, ''What doth baptism signify?'' He read standard works on the subject only to have his difficulties increase; and while teaching school thirty miles from home, he was so wrought upon by a deep spirit of inquiry, that he hired a horse and rode home on Saturday to have his mother show him the authority in the Bible for infant baptism, which he believed some way must be right, but he could not find the authority for it. Reaching home at sundown, he at once began his inquiries, as he must reach his school, thirty miles distant, by school-hour Monday morning. He said:

"Mother, where in the Bible do you find authority for infant baptism?"

She said: "My son, once I had trouble about this subject, but our pastor told me it was all right, and I never have troubled any more about it."

"Mother, that does not satisfy me. I want the scripture authority on which our people justify this rite of the church when confronted by those who do not believe in it."

"Son, you must go to your father."

"Father, where is the authority in the Bible for infant baptism?"

"Why, my son, the Bible is full of it."

"Well, father, put your finger on one place."

"Did you never read the Abrahamic covenant?"

"Yes, father, and I don't find a word of infant baptism in it."

"Go and do as you like."

And this was the sum of argument and information obtained of his best earthly friends on this subject.

Returning to his school, it was not long until he had an opportunity of hearing a traveling Baptist minister preach at a double log house near where he was teaching. After the sermon, supper was prepared and the young teacher invited to stay, which afforded him an opportunity of hearing views entirely new to him. During the conversation, in which young Kincaid sought to display his scholarship, he was twice asked: "And are are you not yet satisfied on the subject of baptism?" An answer was evaded each time, when the preacher said:

"Do you want to read anything further on the subject?"

To which the reply was made:

"If I can find something good and authoritative."

The preacher took from his saddle-pockets a little volume and laid it on the table by the searcher after truth, who looked at the book, then at the preacher, again at the book to assure himself that he was not mistaken; then, looking the preacher full in the face, said:

"Sir, you must have made a mistake; this is only a New Testament."

The preacher replied:

"Young man, if you want any better authority on the subject of baptism than that given by the Holy Ghost, don't come to me."

After passing his four-score years, Dr. Kincaid would relate this story with interest and delight, as it was the first Baptist service he had ever attended, and said he would just as soon have thought of becoming a Shaking Quaker as a Baptist, whom he was accustomed to hear spoken of as a narrow-minded, bigoted and unlettered people, without influence or standing.

But one thing he could not get round. The man seemed to make God's word supreme authority, and it was his one desire to have a scripture reason for all he did or believed.

Learning that a little Baptist colony had located just beyond the settlements in western New York, after his school had closed he made his way to the home of the settled pastor of this little flock in the forest. He found the pastor hoeing among the stumps and green roots preparatory to planting some early garden seed. He asked the pastor for

the scripture authority for infant baptism, and was
plainly and promptly told there was "no scripture
authority for it." "Well, I want to talk with
you. The hoe was dropped, we went into the
house and I learned more theology from that man
in one hour than I had learned in all my life up to
this time." Becoming thoroughly convinced what
was right and duty in the premises, young Kincaid
said: "Well, I want you to baptize me." The
pastor stepped towards the door, took down an
old-fashioned tin bugle, blew it, sat down and
continued the conversation without stopping to
explain. But the candidate was not held very
long in suspense, as the little church soon came
flocking together to answer the bugle-call of their
leader. They heard the experience of the candidate and he was approved for baptism. But never
accustomed to such procedure, and having no
settled views on the subject of baptism when he
went there, had not provided a change of raiment.
So it was arranged that the preacher should go to
the town where Kincaid was studying with his
former Presbyterian pastor, preach, and administer
the ordinance of baptism. This programme was
carried out, and Eugenio Kincaid was baptized at

the age of eighteen years at DeKalb, New York, following the first baptist sermon ever preached in the place.

It was an occasion easily remembered, for the additional reason that his former pastor, with whom he was boarding to secure the use of his Greek and Latin text books, early next morning denied him further use of his library or any further help.

The work of the previous day had brought to young Kincaid a friend in the person of a physician in DeKalb. To him the young convert turned for counsel, and, after some consultation, it was determined that young Kincaid should go one hundred and sixty miles north to Prof. Daniel Haskell's, who had under his instruction at that time Jonathan Wade. Young Kincaid made his parents a short visit and, on the ninth day after his baptism, set out on foot, with his earthly possessions tied up in a handkerchief and twenty-five cents in his pocket, to make the best use of the powers of his whole being for God and the world's salvation. He chopped wood to pay for his lodging and meals on the way, and arrived at his destination without any reverses, in good health and fine spirits. But was quite a little crestfallen

on asking Prof. Haskell for the privilege of studying under him and paying his way in work, to find
all such demands were met in the person of Jonathan Wade, now on the ground.   But when he
related how he had been advised by the kind
physician, the day following his baptism, to make
this journey, and was denied further use of such
books as were needed, Prof. Haskell's large heart
responded: "My boy, I will take you, and we will
do the best we can."   So Eugenio Kincaid became
the second student under Prof. Haskell, and grad-
uated with the first class from the Theological
Seminary at Hamilton, N. Y.

During his course of study at Hamilton the
spirit that led him to cry out on the morning after
his baptism, "Lord, what wilt thou have me to
do?" ripened into deeper convictions of duty to
the heathen, so that he was ready at once to offer
himself to the Baptist Board of Missions, requesting an appointment to Burma.   But the time had
not fully come, and wisely he followed the guiding
hand of providence to mission work in the fields
at home, until the wider door should open.

He was ordained at Westmoreland during his
course of study, and supplied the church there for a

time, but desiring a wider field he first accepted
the pastorate of the First Church at Galway, N. Y.,
where the people became much attached to him
during the three years of a very successful pastorate.   Pleasantly situated as he was with a people
who loved him, he longed to work in the waste
places, so in 1826 he made an exploring tour in
the valley of the Susqehanna, and finding great
destitution, the field was more in keeping with his
longings of soul, and his pleasant pastorate was
readily given up for this, to him, most inviting
field this side of Burma.

"At this time there were not more than two or
three Baptists in all that region; and when calling
at the house of one of these, he introduced himself as a Baptist minister, the old man was quite
overcome, and without making any reply, in an
audible voice thanked God for this long-desired
blessing.   Stated preaching was commenced at
Milton, Union county, and in less than six months
time a church was organized with nine members.

Here in Milton was headquarters, but his field
of labor was in the valley—in the villages and
homes destitute of gospel privileges.   At Warriors
Run a minister of another denomination warned

the people not to hear that young "Baptist preacher," for "Baptist sentiments were the worst of heresies, for once they entered a place they could never be rooted out."

Aside from preaching, *The Literary and Evangelical Register*, a monthly magazine, was edited and published at Milton for a year.

In 1828 an appointment was tendered young Kincaid by the Board of the General Association of Pennsylvania, as its missionary to travel and preach in several of the central counties of the State. His efforts from the very beginning were crowned with success. The secretary says: "In concluding our report we wish to express our high sense of the valuable services rendered by our Brother Kincaid, in whose resignation the Association sustains a great loss. As a pioneer we know not his equal."

In the four years of service for the General Association of Pennsylvania he traveled more than 20,000 miles, exploring the State and preaching in its most destitute places; often he went where no messenger had gone before with the glad tidings of peace.

The night before leaving for India he wrote to the Board as follows:

"The deep interest I have felt in the advancement of the cause in Pennsylvania can never be erased from my mind. My happiness has been identified with the prosperity of the mission cause in that State, and though I may never visit it again, the recollections of past years will ever be present with me. In mind I shall often visit those mountains and valleys where I have so frequently preached the things concerning the Kingdom of God."

Now the wisdom of God seems plain in binding so closely the hearts of the people at home to one so worthy and so able to represent them and their Master abroad. I feel that I should do him an injustice to keep back from the reader some of the hardships of his school life, as well as fail to encourage many a poor boy in school who may think his lot a hard one while pinched with poverty in the school course.

Aside from earning all to pay his way through school—at that time letters were not prepaid as now, but were sent to be paid for on delivery, and instead of the cheap postage of this age, the post-

age on a single letter was twenty-five cents.
Young Kincaid's mother was one of the kindest
of women, and as other mothers loved most tenderly her first-born; and while she may not have
endorsed fully his change of views and church
relations, she nevertheless was faithful in her
prayers for him and correspondence with him. He
was among strangers, and most naturally would
appreciate a kind letter from home. The letter
was there in the post office, and it was from
mother, but the postmaster dare not deliver the
letter without his twenty-five cents. The closest
search reveals not a penny in the schoolboy's
purse, and still worse, no chance to earn postage
money until after the close of the school term,
which was, in more than one instance, a whole
quarter. So that the letters from his mother were
sometimes more than three months old when read,
although but one hundred and sixty miles from
home.

With our prepaid daily mail service and free
delivery system, with the possibility of sandwich-
ing in between mails a telegram, we do not stop
to think how far we are removed from the perplexing delays, inconveniences and expense of

communication when young Kincaid was a schoolboy.

These letters from his mother were kept and so fondly cherished, that he regarded their destruction the most bitter experience of his missionary life. At the outbreak of a war between England and Burma, Dr. Kincaid and his family took refuge on an English merchant vessel, and his embarcation took place so suddenly that the table was left standing on the floor with dinner well-nigh ready to be eaten. After an absence of about three years he returned and found the cherished letters from his mother and a considerable portion of his library worked up into cartridges; and while the English government made an exception in his case and paid him for his books destroyed, the letters were an irreparable loss, that could only be mourned without remedy.

Before further notice of the labors of our zealous and devoted young Christian brother, let us look, in the next chapter, at some of the elements and traits of character in his make-up.

CHAPTER II.

ELEMENTS OF CHARACTER.

"Every work that he begun . . . he did it with all his
heart and prospered."—*2d Chron., xxxi-21.*

For nobler purpose was he born
  Than statesman, lord or king.
To stamp his impress on the world,
  To God much people bring.
No granite shaft could ever tell
  How deep his soul did move,
'Till broke at last the magic spell
  That held back Jesus' love;
And millions once in heathen night
  God's love began to know—
To live in peace with joy and light,
  And on to glory go.

"Many men seem to have no individuality, even though enjoying what is called *reputation*. They are wholly wanting in what constitutes a distinct character. Neither their mental nor their moral attributes are marked by anything that can be regarded as permanent, and but for a certain 'vain show' they would pass through life scarcely challenging recognition. There are others, however, endowed with such gifts that it matters not where they may be placed their presence and influence are seen and felt.

Nor is it difficult to discern the qualities which generally give to individuals position and power.

In all such cases it will be found that the constituent elements of the mind are such as to impart a decided character to all they say and do, and by the confidence with which they speak their sentiments, and the boldness with which they execute their plans they speedily establish a title to pre-eminence even among illustrious associates."

"These natural traits have been strikingly exhibited in the life and labors of Mr. Kincaid, and to their possession must be traced one of the chief causes of his astonishing success."

To exhibit these traits is a difficult "task, in referring to a character so marked by Christian and manly virtues, however, nothing, of course, will be expected beyond a brief outline of the chief qualities for which he became so widely distinguished."

"The *intellectual* endowments of Mr. Kincaid, though not of the first or highest order, were unquestionably far above mediocrity, and the

depth and breadth of their development, under
the circumstances" that surrounded him afford
proof of their native scope and vigor. With contemplative mind, discriminating in its movements,
his mental processes were concluded with great
rapidity and accuracy.

Hence, notwithstanding the time given to active
labors, he was astonishingly successful in acquir-
ing a very large fund of general knowledge. Besides
enjoying a liberal education in his appropriate
sphere, few men were more familiar than he with
the current history of the world, whether in poli-
tics or religion, and the habits of his earlier life
of reading and storing his mind were kept up until
the very last year of his long and useful life.

The wonderful resources possessed within himself "in his good sense, quick sagacity, generous sensibility and fertile imagination were no less
valuable in his declining years than during his
more active life.

"These powers appeared to great advantage on
the platform when under excitement, induced by
crowded audiences, he was portraying the thrilling scenes connected with his labors in Burma, or
when, with strong argument and melting pathos,

he was heard pleading with the churches in behalf of the perishing heathen."

"At such times, a whole assembly has been not only suffused with tears, but so thrilled by his graphic sketches, or so overwhelmed by his impetuous appeals that the feelings of many have found utterance in involuntary, half-suppressed ejaculations."

The *physical* organization of Mr. Kincaid was scarcely less remarkable than his mental developments, and doubtless contributed much towards making up all the other elements of his manhood. In person he was about medium height, firmly though not stoutly built, a remarkable combination of nervous and muscular energy. As the natural result of such a formation constituting the basis of an active temperament, on all occasions he exhibited great powers of endurance, while with a constitution less vigorous he could never have survived the toils and perils through which he passed.

"The action of strong character demands something firm in its natural basis, just as massive engines require solid bearings from which to work."

"This constitutional firmness may at least be regarded as an essential condition to *physical courage.*"

And among the many qualities requisite to the position of "Foreign Missionary" this in his time was one of very great importance.

"In the prosecution of his work" he was often thrown into surroundings where timidity and irresolution would have been ruin. "He therefore needed, in an eminent degree, power to meet emergencies and courage to surmount danger,"

The possession of this quality gives the possessor "full use of his faculties for the prudent and prompt adoption of means to ends, and is one of the rarest and most important of human endowments."

Indeed, without a measure of such courage one can scarcely hope to succeed in any important undertaking because, as Foster said,—"In almost all plans of great enterprise, a man must systematically dismiss at the entrance every wish to stipulate with his destiny for safety." "He voluntarily treads within the precincts of danger; and though it be possible he may escape, he ought to be prepared with the fortitude of a self-devoted victim." "This is the inevitable condition on which heroes, travelers, or missionaries among savage nations, and reformers on a grand scale must commence their careers."

"This dauntless spirit, which is demanded in entering upon a great and hazardous enterprise, is not less essential to its successful prosecution. Here we discover one of the strongest elements, perhaps, in Mr. Kincaid's character; for while quick to perceive, and bold to plan, he was at the same time persevering and confident in execution. He furnished a remarkable illustration of a strenuous will, accompanying the conclusions of thought constantly inciting the utmost efforts to bring about practical results.

"It mattered not how formidable the difficulties, or how persistent the opposition which sought to defeat his plans, so inflexible was the temper of his mind, and so indomitable his courage, that such circumstances only increased the intensity of his soul, and with a feeling bordering onto impunity, he seemed almost to make his way through impossibilities, and reached at last the full execution of his purposes.

"Closely allied with this trait of character was

that of *independence*. Let it cost what it might, he would be honest to the convictions of his own mind, and without stopping to consider what he might lose or what he might gain by any particular course of action, his single inquiry was, What is right? and having satisfied his conscience on this point, without the slightest regard for man's frown or favor he did what he conscientiously believed to be proper and right."

"The rule of his life was to act, so far as possible, from convictions superior to his own passions; and being governed by views of duty too deep and strong to yield to those influences which too often lead men to act in a way which their better judgments would forbid, his course in some instances may have seemed indiscreet, savoring, perchance, of harshness and arrogance."

"Frankly independent in his opinions, however, and not without what would be called strong prejudices—no uncommon feature of powerful minds —Mr. Kincaid was never the man to play the sycophant, nor under any circumstances to feign himself what he was not, and a more perfectly out-spoken and transparent soul" is seldom if ever met than he was.

"In truth, 'my love doth so approve him that even his stubbornness, his checks, and his frowns had grace and favor in them.'

"If anything was needed to temper this independence and guard it against abuse," it was found in his devotion to the Master's cause.

"He possessed to an eminent degree the spirit of him 'who pleased not himself' but said My meat and drink is to do the will of him who sent me and to finish his work."

He gave himself without reserve to the Master's work relinquishing all else that was dear to him and in a spirit of true self denial, brought into captivity every passion of his soul to the obedience of Christ.

"Having fully surrendered himself he was content to derive all his happiness in ceaseless toil for the glory of God and the salvation of men."

Hence while his natural courage supported him amid dangers, oppositions and perils were not able to disturb his self reliance. This feeling of his soul caused him to look to a higher object and enabled him to say with the apostle: "Neither count I my life dear unto myself, so that I might finish my course with joy, and the ministry which

I received of the Lord Jesus, to testify the gospel of the grace of God.''

The spirit of his devotion was the answer to the prayer of the poet:

Give me a heart, O God, to love,
  And seek the good of souls,
Both rich, and poor, of every land
  Between the distant poles.

A holy zeal, O Lord, to grasp
  And shelter at my side
The meanest outcast of the race
  For whom my Savior died.

A heart, dear Savior, that shall love
  The rich, the proud, the vain,
And zeal to plead, with *all* to seek
  Life through a Savior slain.

A heart, O God, to love all men
  Whom Thou hast loved so well,
And strength to plead as Thou didst plead
  To save a world from Hell.

Give heart, to love, and toil and pray,
  And thank Thee for Thy grace ;
Faith to believe, Thou wilt redeem,
  And save our ruined race.

''The secret of his power and success is traceable to his wonderful faith in God's purpose to use him, and the abiding presence of the Holy Spirit with him.''

Says a gifted writer—'The man of faith is a decided character, the instinct of his reason is a strong will, from a strong motive.' He commits his ways to God and says 'I will walk worthy of my vocation. I will be a loyal child of God. The Almighty allows and grants what such a mind wishes.'

"A man without a determined, final faith, an undoubting trust in the true God, is but as a dry leaf on the wings of the wind, carried about by impulses unresisted and unavoidable. As the leaf cannot take root, and rests but to rot, so the faithless man has no living power in him to draw vigor and beauty from the elements.

There is no settled hope without faith—no going forth of the prophetic and realizing soul into the undiscovered depths of space; searching for new evidences and the deeper love of an Omniscient Father, without whose notice, not a sparrow falls to the ground.

Mr. Kincaid exemplified a wonderful and most precious faith in his life to its very close. And we deem it fitting to close this chapter in the well chosen words of Mrs. Luther, who says of him, "Dear, noble old man, hero of a hundred fights, his courage never failed him, whether facing the robbers in northern Burma, or the governor at

Rangoon with his infuriated soldiery, or the terrors of the ecclesiastical council at Maulmain.
Right was right and duty was duty, and his voice
was always heard on the side of right.''

CHAPTER III.

THE FOREIGN MISSIONARY.

"Go ye into all the world, and preach the gospel to every creature."—*Mark xvi, 15.*

Send with Thy word, O God, in hand,
　　And hearts all filled with richest grace,
Those who may preach in every land
　　Salvation to our ruined race.

O help them bear Thy name unheard
　　To millions wrapped in darkest night,
And lead the erring through Thy word,
　　To Christ, the way, the life, the light.

Yes, send, O God, by whom Thou wilt,
　　Just so salvation's message fly,
To save through blood of Jesus spilt,
　　Those who if left alone must die.

"The field in which Mr. Kincaid had for several years been laboring as Home Missionary, and from which abundant harvests had been gathered, was still full of promise, and on every hand he saw most cheering evidences of the divine blessing on his labors." But he heard the call of the Master so distinctly that his heart responded most cheerfully. In the language of another:

Lord, in this hour of urgent need,
   Send me to some dark field,
To sow broadcast the precious seed
   That golden fruit may yield.

Though thorns infest the rocky soil,
   They are not plants of Thine ;
There help me, Lord, with ceaseless toil
   To sow Thy truth divine.

Send Thou the dew, the heat, the rain,
   To make each barren field
No longer be a fruitless plain,
   But ripened harvests yield.

Though long I wait, no increase see,
   Lord, help me still to sow,
And leave the increase all to Thee,
   For Thou canst make it grow.

And shall some other reap the grain,
   No difference shall it make,
Since Thou must share each toil and pain,
   I suffer for Thy sake.

Many were content to labor at home, with
friends and comforts on every hand, while but few
had convictions of duty to the heathen, whose
needs so weighed upon him that he could most
cheerfully trust the little churches, fruit of his
first toil, and the promising valley of the Susque-
hanna to the Great Shepherd's care, while his zeal
for the divine glory and his love for the lost fixed
more firmly his purpose of preaching the gospel
to the perishing millions of Burma.

"At length the way opened" and Mr. Kincaid together with Mr. Mason and their wives were publicly set apart to their responsible work on the evening of May 23d, 1830, at the Baldwin Place church in the presence of a crowded audience, Kincaid preaching from 2nd Corinthians xiii, 11, "Finally brethren farewell. Be perfect, be of good comfort, be of one mind, live in peace; and the God of love and peace shall be with you."

"It was an affectionate valedictory, indicating a mind tenderly alive to the best interests of men; and giving proof that while he looked with earnest desire to benefit distant nations, he cherished a deep solicitude for the spiritual welfare of those from whom he was soon to be separated." "At the close of the sermon, Dr. Bolles, in behalf of the Board, delivered an impressive charge, alluding in appropriate terms to the extensive field of their labor, the difficulties to be encountered, the zeal requisite to the work, the self-denial which such service demanded, and the pleasing encouragements presented of ample reward here, and of an eternal reward hereafter, as the result of their toils." "Then, with the aspect and style of fraternal and Christian affection for which he was so remark-

able," "Rev. Mr. Knowles presented to them
the hand of fellowship, accompanying the act with
cheering words and pledging to them the fervent
prayers of the churches for their safety and ulti-
mate success." "On the following morning at 5
o'clock, just previous to the time of sailing, a
prayer-meeting was held at the First Baptist meet-
ing-house, where a large assembly met to unite in
seeking the presence and blessing of the Lord to
accompany his servants across the bosom of the
deep and in the land of the heathen."

"At the close of this meeting, sorrowing, yet
rejoicing, Dr. Kincaid took a final and affectionate
leave of his brethren, adverting briefly to the deep
sensibility which parting with Christian friends
excited, but declaring that he felt unspeakably
happy in prospect of so soon entering upon labors
connected with the diffusion of the knowledge of
the Savior among those who were sitting in the
region and shadow of death."

"Mrs. Kincaid then spoke in a very tender,
touching manner of how she had sighed for an
opportunity of instructing the Burmese women
and how she rejoiced at the prospect of soon realizing her hopes, and in behalf of Mrs. Mason pro-

fessed a readiness, heartily to co-operate with their husbands in missionary labors."

"After prayer by Rev. Mr. Choules, the assembly with the missionaries repaired to the ship and on the wharf united in singing"—

" Ye messengers of Christ,
    His sovereign voice obey ;
Arise ! and follow where He leads,
    And peace attend your way.

The Master whom ye serve,
    Will needful strength bestow ;
Depending on His promised aid,
    With sacred courage go.

Mountains shall sink to plains,
    And hell in vain oppose ;
The cause is God's and must prevail,
    In spite of all His foes.

Go, spread a Savior's fame ;
    And tell His matchless grace,
To the most guilty and depraved,
    Of Adam's num'rous race.

We wish you in His name,
    The most divine success ;
Assur'd that He who sends you forth
    Will your endeavors bless."

" Dr. Bolles, the corresponding secretary, then led in devout supplication to heaven for a prosperous voyage, that the winds and the waves might be propitious, and the seamen participate in the blessings of the gospel, after which mutual saluta-

tions were exchanged, and the missionaries
embarked on board the *Martha*, Capt. Lovett, for
Calcutta.''

''As the vessel left its moorings, a solemn still-
ness prevailed among the crowd of spectators,
broken only by the smothered sobs of those who
wept over the separation, and every heart sent up
a silent, earnest prayer to that gracious and
Almighty Being, who holds the winds 'by His
might' and the ocean in the hollow of His hand,
that he would not only waft them safely over the
deep, but give them an open and effectual door
among the heathen, and crown, with abundant
success, all their efforts to shed over Burma the
saving light of truth.

Soon the vessel began to fade in the distance,
and when straining eyes could no longer recognize
the features of those on board, slowly they left the
dock and returned to their several homes.

What the feelings of the departing missionaries
were, may easily be imagined, though they have
never been written. The ship was soon plunging
her bows into the white-crested billows, and when
the last dim outline of their native land disappeared from view, O with what sadness of

heart did they retire to their lonely cabin! Now, as never before, they began to realize their situation. They had renounced the comforts and privileges of a refined and Christian land to dwell among rude heathen.

Every tender tie known to earth had been sundered, and having parted with fond parents, with loved brothers and sisters, and with happy circles of sympathizing Christian friends, they now felt, more keenly, the sundering of those endearing associations, stronger than iron bands, the breaking of which well nigh sank their spirits within them."

In like circumstances Mrs. Judson wrote in her Journal:

"Still my heart bleeds. O America! my native land! Must I leave thee? Must I leave my parents, my sister and brother, my friends beloved, and all the scenes of my early youth; * * where I learned the endearments of friendship and tasted all the happiness this world can afford; where I learned also to value a Savior's blood and count all things but loss in comparison with the knowledge of Him! Yes, I must leave you all, for a heathen land and an uncongenial clime. Fare-

4

well, happy, happy scenes, but never, no never, to be forgotten."

"It was in that hour of conflict with nature that the missionaries bowed together in prayer, looked alone to God for strength and were comforted."

They prayed for strength all storms to brave.
 And that salvation like a wave,
Should cover all the land of night
 As does the sun with warmth and light.

That God should nearer to them be
 In home and work across the sea,
Enfold them in His arms of power
 And shield them in each trying hour.

That when the race of life is run
 And sinks the soul like setting sun,
They like the sun at break of day
 May each the love of God display.

By coming robed in spotless white,
 Where rich, resplendent love and light
Flow out to fill the vaulted skies,
 Where praises evermore shall rise.

Till like the mighty thunder's roar,
 Heaven is moved from shore to shore,
So mighty is the praise we'll sing
 To Jesus Christ, our Lord and King.

CHAPTER IV.

ENTERING ONTO HIS LIFE WORK.

In safety Dr. Kincaid reached Calcutta, September 30, 1830, from whence he embarked to Maulmain, arriving there Sunday morning, November 28th, and wrote:

"We gazed upon the scenery around us with feelings not easily described." As the rays of the sinking sun, mellowed with the twilight and "the dark field spread out before us, with its mountains and plains and, rivers and vales, and its mighty population enveloped in a moral gloom that cast dark shadows over this portion of the globe, we felt more than ever for the missionaries who had toiled and suffered on these shores, and we had enlarged views of the work before us." Dear reader, how we should praise God for the change that has exceeded the conception of Dr. Kincaid as he thought of the work of Christ in Burma. He said, "Paganism will yield to the power of the gospel of the Son of God, who shall make the desert to blossom as the rose.

At this time there were two churches in Burma, with fierce opposition on the part of the priesthood.   But Dr. Kincaid began at once the study of the language, preaching at the same time to the British soldiers of the Forty-fifth regiment, who provided a commodious house of worship.

"On the assemblies convened in this chapel God, in a signal manner, poured out his spirit.   Converts were multiplied and the church grew strong.

Of this wonderful work of grace Dr. Kincaid wrote: "Many a giant that defied the armies of the living God has fallen; not to perish, but to be raised to life everlasting."   This was indeed a time of refreshing from the presence of the Lord with constant ingathering of souls.   "Many who came to scoff went away agonizing under the awakening influence of the Holy Spirit."

As one result of this revival, about one hundred souls were baptized into the little church.

In March, Dr. Kincaid, accompanied by Mr. Wade, made a tour of two hundred or three hundred miles up the Martiban river, visiting the Kárens, who were quite numerous, and they were permitted to baptize nine persons.   On returning, he wrote:

"During our absence we have seen much of the goodness of God, and have had increasing evidence that the Lord has much people in idolatrous Burma to be called out of darkness into the glorious light of the gospel. Surely the fields are white for the harvest, and the urgency of preaching the gospel to the heathen gathers force at every step we take. How delightful and encouraging to see poor, blind heathen recovering the light of life."

At that time little was known of the Karens, a numerous and interesting people in the Burman Empire. They were found to be milder mannered and more industrious than the Burmans, exceedingly superstitious and without fixed religious principles.

They were wholly ignorant of the use of medicine, and supposed the missionaries possessed of skill superior to the Nats, the source to which they attributed all evils that befell them. They brought their sick to the missionary, and were delighted with the results of the medicine given. And the work was rapidly opening to the gleaner's hand, when clouds of sorrow began to arise indicative of new and sorer trials than hitherto had crossed the path of Dr. Kincaid. His wife, who had been

studying the language and managing a school, was
attacked by a disease peculiar to the climate, and
which so reduced her strength that all hopes of her
recovery soon fled.   Their boy, born November
10th, only tarried until December 8th, and quit
his stay on earth for realms of glory, whither the
freed spirit of his mother followed eleven days
later.   Dr. Kincaid's own words may best describe
the depth of this double bereavement, and how
God was with him through it all.

"It becomes my painful duty to give a detailed
account of the most afflicting events of my whole
life.   Hitherto I have been a stranger to sorrow—
the cup of affliction has been dealt out to me with
a sparing hand.   My family was dearer to me than
my own life, and a residence on this side the waste
of waters, far from kindred and friends, has served
to endear them an hundred fold; separated as we
were from the land of our fathers, and surrounded
by thousands of poor ignorant heathen, our own
humble home became a world of itself; together
we wept and prayed around the family altar, and
together labored for the acquisition of that language
by which we might communicate the glorious gospel
to the millions of Burma."   "But now I am left

to make my way alone on these heathen shores."

The companion and wife of his youth had followed her babe, and was done with earthly toil and care.

Alone now, he must weep and pray. Her prayers and weeping forevermore were ended. Dear reader, if you do not know what it is, as you may learn what it means to see the cold, damp death-sweat gathering on affection's fairest brow, and the eyes set, the lips stilled, think of the servant of God, thousands of miles from his native home and loved ones, "watching *all* that was lovely in life fading and withering under the influence of a deadly disease. "Tears of unavailing sorrow" may fall but they give little comfort to the stricken and lonely heart. "After we arrived in India we were blessed with excellent health, until the rainy season began, then we had a slight attack of intermittent fever, but after about ten days it left me, without taking medicine. Not so with Mrs. Kincaid. She had this fever at intervals, accompanied by bowel complaint, both of which were relieved, only to be followed by a more fatal malady, "peculiar to the climate and very fatal to foreigners."

"Our little babe took sick on the 5th, and continued sinking until the 8th, when it went into convulsive fits; from the first of which it recovered, but a few hours later went into a second one and expired."

"Mrs. Kincaid sat in a chair and held him in the last fit, notwithstanding "I begged her for my sake and hers not to exert herself; but a mother's affection prevailed over her better judgment. However, when she saw that its emancipated spirit had taken its upward flight, she became calm, and felt so well satisfied that it was all for the best, that she often told me that she had not one desire that her sweet babe should be restored to her again. This resignation to the will of God was given us in mercy. November 1st I had laid aside my books, stopping all work, "except to preach in English, and made it my whole business, night and day, to administer to her wants." "Lord's day, December 18th, I perceived that the disease was rapidly approaching a fatal crisis. "After considerable conversation I told her it was time for meeting, and that I had one person to baptize; she said 'very well, but you will return as soon as possible.' I was back before twelve o'clock, and we had as much conversation as her strength would permit. "After

preaching again in the evening, on the subject,"
'For our light afflictions which are but for a
moment,' etc. "We both felt that this probably
would be the last evening we should spend together
on earth." "I told her that this separation to me
was awfully painful, but I perceived it to be the
will of God." She said her hope was 'in Christ,'
but she had not that cheering prospect she wished.
Yet she felt weaned from the world, and could
leave her family in the hands of God." Similar
statements were made at intervals until 11 o'clock
in the evening, when "she urged me to lie down
a little time and rest. At one o'clock when I arose
I saw she was fast going—"gave her some laven-
der, which revived her, and she fell into an easy
sleep until about two o'clock, when she awoke and
said to me with a clear voice, 'I am now dying,'
and, raising her eyes, continued silent." "I applied
some restoratives to her temples, but soon perceived
the cold, clammy sweat of death gathering on her
forehead. After a little time a heavenly smile
came over her countenance, and more of the divine
presence I never felt;" "there was something
friendly in the approach of death, and with pleasure
I could have unrobed myself and descended with

my dear companion into the dark valley. Heaven seemed to be just at hand, and the glories of the eternal world rose in delightful and awful majesty before me." "Never before did I feel such strength in prayer; never before such entire consecration to the will of God." "I stood in silent, watchful attention to see the spirit fling its last look on the world and wing its way" to a mansion in glory. "After this she did not speak, but continued looking upwards, with a countenance that indicated that she had caught a glimpse of brighter visions of eternity."

"About four o'clock in the morning, December 19th. She resigned her spirit without a struggle or groan. When I saw that all was over I called a Burman female, who was sleeping in an adjoining room, and said to her in the Burman language, the teacher is dead. The sound awoke little Wade, and, springing from his bed, he cried out in the most heartrending manner, 'Is my ma dead?' 'Is my ma dead?' and for a time was inconsolable."

"Few children of his age ever received more instruction from a parent. During the last six or eight months his dear ma had labored much to instruct him in the knowledge of religion, and often took him alone and prayed for him. "Impressions were here made on his mind which I trust were never forgotten."

This hasty narrative of facts will enable those whose households have been broken into by death to sympathize even now with him who now is in realms of glory awaiting the redemption of that body in which he suffered so much that, reunited, the triumph may be complete.

The reader will, I trust, have observed in this chapter two things worthy of special remembrance and study. While perfectly natural for Dr. Kincaid to love his new home a hundred fold more because of its surroundings, and to love his companion more dearly than his own life, an allwise God and loving Father, whom they had gone there together to serve, permitted death to come in and to break up this cherished household, that had come to be "*a world in itself.*" * * * Called the mother and child away to Himself, in such manner as to enable our bereaved brother to trust God more implicitly, and, as he said, have more "strength in prayer than ever before," and to consecrate himself more completely and entirely to Christ and His cause, since these had gone to dwell with Him forever, who purchased them with His own blood.

CHAPTER V.

"A light to lighten the Gentiles."—*Luke, xi-32.*

Spires that gleamed in the brilliant sun,
  So charming the native eye,
Crumble before the work begun,
  And in broken ruins lie.
The Temple of God now sheds its light,
  And drives all darkness away,
And changes the shades of heathen night
  For bright, effulgent, gospel day.

In 1832, while successfully conducting the schools at Rangoon, and yet unable to preach in the Burman tongue, Dr. Kincaid was forced to the conclusion that preaching the gospel must be relied upon as the most potent power man can wield for the salvation of his race. The circulation of Bibles, tracts and religious literature are all important factors, but preaching the gospel to every creature is fulfilling the great commission—is God's chosen method for the overthrow of error and the building of His kingdom among men. More and more was he convinced that the gospel conveyed by the living voice, accompanied by the Spirit's power, was the means of heaven's appointment to which man might look for success, and on which God would show His smile of approval. Every means to awaken and enlighten the conscience was important. But in portraying the power of Jesus' redeeming love—largely in Jesus' own words from the living voice that had known both the power of sin and of God's redeeming love—could the greatest success be hoped for.

After a stay of one year in Rangoon, Dr. Kincaid went to Madras, where he married Miss Barbary McBain, the daughter of a military officer, who shared his toils and sorrows, and stood faithfully by him until he had passed his four score and five years, and answered the call "come up higher."

While absent the schools had been broken up, and those left in charge of the general interest of the mission seized, fined and subjected to great cruelties and punishments.

On his return to Rangoon Dr. Kincaid boldly resumed his labors, and was soon visited by great numbers, both from city and province, especially during the great annual festival of Gaudama. Many came to inquire about the printing press, others about the sciences, while many seemed more concerned about the new religion. Some came as disputants, seeking to entangle the new teacher in his talk, as did the Pharisees our Savior. One of these asked on one occasion :

"Is God without beginning or end, and is he exempt from old age or death?"

"It is true."

"And where is God?"

"In heaven."

"Has God a body?"

"He is a spirit."

"How shall we know this when we cannot see Him?"

"Just as you know you have a soul, though you cannot see the soul with the eyes of the body."

"After death shall we see God?"

"If before death you receive divine light."

"What is it?"

Then several passages of Scripture were cited and read to him in the hearing of the many who stood by, explaining Christ's mission into the world, His death on the cross, His burial, resurrection, and promise of eternal life to all who believe on His name.

He taught them that divine light came through a belief of and in Christ, and by the aid of the Holy Spirit, who reproves the world of sin and leads believers into all truth. To such is given great peace of mind, their darkness gives place to light, and from them the terrors of death are taken away, so that they may sleep as sweetly in the promises of Jesus as the babe in it's mother's arms.

A government man attempted to prove that all religions were alike, but after an earnest effort of about thirty minutes, left in haste, possibly hoping that the crowd would follow him, but instead they looked to the new teacher for a reply. Dr. Kincaid said : "That man has many words, but they give no light," and he taught them by the apt figure of genuine and counterfeit coin that there was a *true*, living and eternal God, and that there are false gods. The true God gave just and good laws, while from false gods might issue many laws which, if observed, would never better the observer's condition. The law of any false god is of no force. It may be so good an imitation of some divine precept in some particulars as to seem possessed of real merit, as the dangerous counterfeit, but when put to the test is discovered to be but imitations, without standard value.   The effort to lead away the crowd on this occasion was futile, and gave good opportunity to set the truth in clearer light.   So, often, interference and attempts to suppress the truth, but give it zest and power.

Sanilaus, who taught Dr. Kincaid the Burman language, and from whom, in turn, he learned of Christ, the mediator between the Eternal God and men, was put into confinement for renouncing his old religion and acknowledging belief in and allegiance to the *true, living* and *Eternal God.*   And as he was a man of great ability and learning, and about to die in his confinement, of a lingering fever, some high official interceded with the king in his behalf, and a very great number of people were called together and Sanilaus was brought forth, with the understanding that if to the question put to him by the king in the presence of his old friends and the multitude brought to bear witness, he should only incline the head so an affirmative answer might be inferred from him by the people, he should be released and go free.   Did he nod assent to the superiority of the religion of Gaudama?   No!   But in fetters and with fever, for his manly answer, "*I believe in the Eternal God,*" went back

to his prison bed and died.   This single act confirmed in more minds that there was real worth in
the new religion than many months of preaching
by the missionaries would have done.

When a little church of eight members had
been formed, a younger brother of the queen was
found among them, and to prevent his attendance
at the preaching and regular services, the queen
compelled this brother to attend her home, and
have charge of the elephant that conveyed her to
the pagoda for idol worship.   After sundown he
was free, and often found his teacher to pour out
his griefs and get courage and strength.   He frequently joined in the family devotions; and to
break him off from these opportunities and the
privileges of the little church, his sister appointed
him governor of a small province some hundreds
of miles distant.   For a time this seemed more
than he could bear.   His grief at being separated
from the white teacher and the little church
weighed him down; but when assured that his
brethren would pray for him, and that God could
be with him and possibly use him more efficiently
as governor than in any other way, he went to his
position, and only a few months had passed when

the priests complained that missionaries had invaded his province, teaching new and strange doctrines. How wisely Providence, by him, opened a wider door for the missionaries and the gospel of the Son of God to come in its mighty saving power to all the province.

Moung-zoo-the, a young man of promising talents and for some time an inquirer, desired baptism and was asked "Are you not afraid to be baptized?"

"I have been, but fear is gone and I feel strong now."   "Perfect love casteth out fear."

"But suppose you are seized, put into prison and beaten with a bamboo; will you be strong then?"

"I cannot deny Christ."

"But suppose they kill you?"

"Let them kill; I desire to follow Christ."

"Whosoever will save his life shall lose it ; but whosoever shall lose his life for my sake and the gospel's, the same shall save it."

Not many were so firm, but allowed the fear of persecution to smother their convictions and deter them from the duty of openly acknowledging Christ; and many attempted to serve God in a

secret way, while still others would come hundreds of miles to learn from the white teacher
about the eternal God, and about his son who died
for all men.

When light broke in on such minds often they
confessed openly and followed at once as the early
disciples.

Favored with such indications of divine help
and blessing, his heart took courage and when
asked by a Burman official how long he intended
to stay in Burma, he might be in a measure
excused for saying, "Until all Burma worships
the eternal God."

He saw, despite the opposition in high places,
the fields whitening to the reaper's hand, converts grew firmer, inquirers more determined, the
leavening influence of gospel power widening on
every hand. These gave him enlarged views of
the work before him.

His faith grew stronger in the God of missions
and in the final overthrow of idolatry in India and
the universal reign of Christ in all the world.

CHAPTER VI.

FROM RANGOON TO AVA.

" Blessed are ye that sow beside all waters."—Isa. xxxii, 20.

Repeated inquiries from friends as to why Dr. Kincaid did not locate at the capital brought to his mind the advantages of that city. It afforded opportunities offered at no other city in the empire.

To avail himself of these opportunities and put himself in a position to do the very most possible good for the cause of Christ in Burma, Dr. Kincaid, with his wife and her sister, both English ladies; Ko Shoon and Ko San-lone, two native preachers, with several other Burmans, embarked for Ava on a Burman boat, April sixth, 1833.

The parting at the riverside with the native Christians was tender and very affecting, revealing the strength of the bonds that bound them together.

The first event of interest on their way was the springing of a leak in their boat and its repair after several hours of unceasing and hard work. The next event worthy of special mention was an

attack by one of the numerous bands of robbers
that infested almost every river village. The
attack was sudden and determined and tried the
nerves of the men, all of whom fled but six,
against whom, with Dr. Kincaid at their head, the
robbers were rushing rapidly, when a "large Burman boat hove in sight." This, together with
Dr. Kincaid's dauntless courage, drove the robbers back in the direction from which they came.

But little thought was given to this close call as
they found opportunities of spreading the gospel
of peace and life among these rude people, and
beholding cheering evidences that some seed found
lodgement, and in time would yield fruit.

"Almost every day witnessed some token of
the divine favor and blessing, for which they gave
thanks and took courage.

In the city of Thir-a-wan many said, we want
to hear more of this religion; if it is true that
there is a God who is free from old age, sickness
and death, he must be the most excellent. Five
men declared their convictions of the truth, and
determined thorough examination.

While Dr. Kincaid was preaching at a village
beyond, a woman who was listening cried out:

"*This God is the True God! This doctrine is the divine communication!* She stated in private conversation afterward that as soon as she *heard*, the *truth* shined upon her mind, she "saw instantly that all her life she had been stupid by worshipping what was no God."

They found opposition to the distribution of books and tracts from the chief secretary of Mey-an-Oung, until he heard some passages read, then he declared that "these books teach the *true God*," and was not satisfied until he had a copy of each kind for himself; and would not allow the missionaries to depart until they had eaten a meal prepared for them.

Another government man directed all his men to ask for books and read about the eternal God. He frankly admitted his doubts about Gaudama's religion, and that these doubts had been increased by hearing two or three great men in Ava declare their convictions of the genuineness of the new religion, and that it would spread. He gave evidence of sincerity and a desire to receive the gospel.

At Poung-day, a city near the size of Rangoon, Dr. Kincaid was invited to the house of the great

Toung-diven, teacher, the head of the most powerful dissenting sect in Burma. On arrival Dr.
Kincaid found a venerable old man, with about
forty others, assembled to hear the conversation.

When asked, "Have you read the word of God?"
the venerable man replied : "I read about a year
ago one small book that reasoned about the Eternal
God and Gaudama."

"What do you think?"

"I have remained careless."

"You are, then, indifferent as to whether you
are right or wrong, and I need say nothing to you."

During a conversation of some length which
followed, the old man expressed anxiety to know
why we went to so much trouble, amid exposure
and reproach, and danger, to publish this new
religion among strangers who cared nothing for
them. Jesus, who died for *all men*, sends his heralds into all the world to preach the gospel of
peace. They are to go alike among all nations—
where prosperity may smile or adversity frown
—amid darkness and danger, or sunlight and peace,
and lead lives of self-denial and faith, that as the
moon throws back its borrowed light upon the
earth, God's ambassadors should throw back upon

the people of earth the light of the Son of Righteousness.   So the missionaries but do their duty
in leading lives of self-denial to save the Burmans
from hell.   The old teacher's interest was such
that he followed Dr. Kincaid to the boat to hear
and get books.

At the town of Sheret, while distributing tracts,
an interesting young man made his way through
the crowd that lined the shores, and asked for a
copy of "St. John's History of Christ and the Acts
of the Apostles."   When asked if he had read
these books he said: "Yes; Teacher Judson gave
them to me in Prome, and in the burning of the
city the books were lost."   When he had received
the books asked for and four tracts, he disappeared,
and we moved our boat about two miles further up
town to shield us from the wind, and while we
thought of the young man, we did not expect to
see him any more, but at nightfall he returned to
the boat and reported another believer in Christ in
the city who wanted to see the teacher and get
books.

Dr. Kincaid followed the young man, and was
almost overjoyed at finding a venerable old man,
full of faith and hope in Christ, though his only

teacher was the gospel of John and the Holy Spirit. For two years he had loved the Savior, and his language attested a heart acquaintance with Jesus. How encouraging to spend a few hours in a great idolatrous city and nation with two such promising disciples. They were firm and outspoken in their expressions of love for and admiration of Jesus.

One man about forty years old, some months before, had read a small book, which he said made known to him the true and living God. At first he was careless, but afterwards was so moved that he feared to worship idols any more, but did not know how to worship the Eternal God. Dr. Kincaid gave him all the Epistles, and told him they were the words of the Most High God, and that he must believe in Christ and pray for divine light.

After traveling about fifty-four days, and visiting about three hundred cities and villages, in most of which they had scattered books and tracts, and had preached the gospel, their perilous voyage was ended, and they slept without the walls of Ava for the night of May 30th.

The friends of missions in two hemispheres had looked with mingled anxiety and fear for the completion of this voyage.

And to-day I distinctly remember hearing Dr. Kincaid relate, after he had passed his four-score years, the anxiety of that night under the shadow of the wall of that great, wicked city. How he wrestled and prayed almost the entire night, and how peace, and comfort and courage came about *four* o'clock in the morning, and peaceful and refreshing slumber came to fit him for his first day's work in the great capital city of the Burman empire.

How eventful that June morning that started Dr. Kincaid and his two native assistants into the great city to turn its idolatrous people from the worship of idols to the worship of the true and living God.

He went from group to group, from place to place, until he had gone between three and four miles along one side of a street, and turning, he retraced his way on the other side of the street, everywhere talking of Jesus as redeemer and mediator between man and the great Eternal God.

Most all heard cautiously, a few with marked attention, but the great masses from curiosity, and I presume now and then an old man, an official who remembered the days and possibly the untold sufferings of Dr. Judson. Prejudice and opposition both began to show themselves at once.

The remembrance of those cruelties to Dr. Judson, the dense population of the city, the activity among officials about the king's court and in military circles, all tended to excite a deeper anxiety in the mind of Dr. Kincaid as he stood alone viewing the field his heart longed to see redeemed from darkness and death to the light and liberty of the gospel, and made loyal to the Lord Jesus.

CHAPTER VII.

OPPOSITION AT THE CAPITAL.

The mighty arms of God's love
Were underneath, around, above,
To shield, to comfort and uphold,
While He the gospel should unfold,
To those in depths of Pagan night ;
Who sought in vain that life and light
Through idol gods of wood and stone
That comes through Jesus Christ alone.

The solicitude felt in the two hemispheres about Dr. Kincaid's reception and safety at the capital gave place to experiences and knowledge of strong opposition and persecution. And he was called upon for the exercise of all that courage and perseverance that so distinguished him in after years. Less courage and indomitable will power and perseverance might have turned away or fled before the opposition at Ava. There were many inviting and promising fields where the opposition would have been less formidable, and the immediate surroundings more promising, but from the capital messages of Jesus could be sent into every province of Burma.

Evidence that Dr. Kincaid should have no royal welcome in the capital was seen in the efforts of the physician to the king to dislodge him from his dwelling by force.

By the efforts of Ko San-lone, a native Christian, a house had been obtained of a lady of nobility and entered without a government permit to rent it. After a residence of three days this lady died, and the house fell into possession of the royal doctor, who dispatched a messenger at once to the missionary ordering him to vacate the premises at once. The next day the royal doctor went in person, was quite uncivil and threatening in his manner, but after a time seemed disposed to reason, and on promise that another house would be provided as quick as possible, seemed to go away satisfied. Efforts were renewed every day to obtain a government permit to rent another house. Four Woon-gees composed the king's first council, and four Atwen-woons his second council. Some one or more of these was seen every day, but they excused the delay every time, and were always prolific with promises.

"Once the young prince's ears must be bored, which occupied eight or nine days." The Chinese

Ambassadors leaving the royal court took up about five days. Four wild elephants were to be caught, which occupied three more days. Thus it went from day to day.

Until one morning when Dr. Kincaid called on Moung-sa, a Woon-gee, and who had been an At-wen-woon when Dr. Judson first went to Ava, his manner and countenance were changed.

Silently the servant of God waited to hear the worst — not able to conjecture the cause of the cold reception, with probable thought of the death prison and iron fetters, sufferings and tortures of Dr. Judson and wife on this field with the gospel, when this man was one of the king's second council.

The Woon-gee soon broke the silence, however, by saying: "The king is pained to hear that in Rangoon, and in all the cities and villages along the river, you have given books and preached to the people."

"It is not agreeable to the king to have a new doctrine spread among his subjects. He has given orders that the English and American doctrine spread no further."

Dr. Kincaid replied :

"I am a teacher of religion. Can I not preach to the people?"

"Yes, but you must not give books. Why do you not preach to the Mussulmen and Catholics?"

"I came to Ava to preach to *all* people of whatever nation, and if not allowed to do so, shall leave the city and go to some other nation."

This nobleman had a real or feigned aversion to foreigners, which at times he took little pains to conceal.

As stated earlier, the royal doctor, on parting with Dr. Kincaid, seemed willing to wait until another house could be secured, but on the following day he sent his furniture, with an order to put it into the house.

They were forbidden to do this, whereupon the royal doctor soon appeared, with about twenty young men, to execute his order to put his furniture into the house and Dr. Kincaid's into the street.

All attempts at reasoning were vain. Two young men rushed to the top of the stairway to seize Dr. Kincaid, who shoved them back and barred the door. In the afternoon Ko San-lone, who had been in search of a house, returned. He was seized and

thrown down by the royal doctor, and pounced
upon by several of the young men.

Dr. Kincaid could not hear his cries and endure
such cruelties inflicted on his faithful servant. He
unbarred the door, and, with a large cane in hand,
rushed out, threatening them.   Instantly they let
go Ko San-lone and, with pointed bamboos and
Burman spears, rushed upon Dr. Kincaid like
young tigers. Five of them were felled to the
ground, the door again barred, and the royal doctor
for the first time ready to reason.   Whereupon the
door was thrown open, and the royal doctor was an
invited guest, and said he had been very angry,
had behaved badly, and begged Dr. Kincaid to
forget it.

The British resident, hearing these facts, caused
the royal doctor to be placed in stocks, and sent a
man each day to see that his royalty did not screen
him from justice.

Soon Dr. Kincaid procured another house near
the heart of the city, where he was permitted to
see the same earnest spirit of inquiry manifest itself
that had cheered him all along the Irrawaddy.

The gospel leaven was at work, and the smothered flame could not be kept down long.   Too

many had felt the Spirit's quickening power.
Resistance and threats were now in vain. In
defiance of the proposition to hang six or eight of
the natives about the veranda of Dr. Kincaid's
house and leave them there until their bodies
rotted away, to deter the people from gathering
there to hear the gospel, hundreds went daily,
among them many government men and high
officials, some, perhaps, as spies, others as Nico-
demus, to inquire by night after the truth.

Having begun to preach the gospel there, Dr.
Kincaid said there was no going back nor working
quietly or in the dark.   One course only could be
pursued, and that was to preach Christ to all classes
and leave results with God.   Though forbidden to
preach or disseminate in any way the knowledge
of Jesus, and often summoned to appear before
courts, Dr. Kincaid was conscious of the increasing
favor of the gospel with the multitudes, and its
growing power on those who embraced it.

On the 22nd of March, 1834, Dr. Kincaid was
summoned to appear before the *High Court* of the
empire.   When he reached the royal court one of
the Woon-gees sternly demanded of Dr. Kincaid
why he had come to the royal city.   His answer

6

was to diffuse abroad the knowledge of Jesus.

"Dare you say the religion of the king, his princes and his nobles and his people is false?"

"I do not say so, but in my own country, and in all the world before the knowledge of the living God appeared, the people worshiped idols, and the command of God is to 'Go into all the world and preach' this religion."

"Stop; it is not proper to say so much. It is the wish of the king, his ministers and myself that you preach no more."

"If you send us away the whole world will ridicule you. Why, my lord, are you afraid of two men?"

"We do not want you here. Go to Rangoon."

Much conversation similar to the above took place, toward the close of which he was more gentle and less haughty, but utterly refused to reason.

After eight months Dr. Kincaid was again summoned before the high court. All the noblemen and an immense throng of the common people were gathered at the great court, and when Dr. Kincaid entered the room the great *Black Book* was brought out and chapter after chapter read, attempting a portrayal of Dr. Kincaid's character.

It was penned in the Black Book that the *American teacher* had come to the Golden City, had stirred up great numbers of the people to despise the gods and religion of Burma ; disturbed the public peace and preached a law they could not approve. No voice was heard but that of the reader, until a passage was read declaring, "About seven months before the American teacher had promised neither to preach nor to give books away any more, and disregarding this promise, he had given books in every direction and gone on preaching.

Dr. Kincaid could not be silent longer, but said: "I never heard of such a promise before. I promised to give no more of the Investigator, and the Woon-gees gave me permission to preach and give the sacred scriptures."

A Woon-gee angrily said, "We know nothing about your books. You promised to give *no books.*

They then demanded the promise that he would preach no more nor give any more books of any kind.

Dr. Kincaid replied :

"I dare not promise."

"You must promise," retorted one of the council.

"I cannot; I dare not make such a promise. I
fear God more than men; and if you cut off both
my arms and then my head, I cannot make such a
promise."

"Remain quiet and you can stay," said one of
milder manner.

"I dare not remain quiet. I came here to preach,
and the command of God is to preach in all the
world."

Furious shouts from half a dozen said, "Send
him away; he is not fit to live in the Empire."

Dr. Kincaid then appealed to the queen's brother,
who listened respectfully until reference was made
to the expense of renting a house. This, said the
prince, shall be refunded to you.

One of the ministers said: If we do not oppose
you we shall go to hell. We dare not listen to you.

As I ponder and pen these trials of the "Hero
Missionary," more and more can I see the wisdom
of God in refusing me work on a foreign field, for
years the most ardent wish of my life. There is
within me a conscious lack of that *grace* and *grit*
so often needed in the moulding period of the
mission churches in the days of Judson, Vinton
and Kincaid.

Knowing Dr. Kincaid as intimately as I came to know him, the last six years of his earthly life, it seems plain to me why God sent him, to plant and train a little church in the Golden City of the Burman Empire.

CHAPTER VIII.

THE GOSPEL AT AVA.

" Be not afraid, but speak and hold not thy peace ; for
I am with thee, and no man shall set on thee to hurt thee ;
for I have much people in this city."—*Acts xviii, 9.*

What reviving news we hear,
　　Words of comfort, full of cheer,
How the gospel wins the day
　　In that city far away.

In the centre of that land,
　　Where pagodas thickly stand,
Jesus now is sought and owned,
　　Idols too are there dethroned,

Jesus doth in Ava stay,
　　O'er the Empire gaining sway,
In the land His name is known
　　As King *all* nations ought to own.

The labors of Dr. Kincaid at Ava were attended
with a variety of difficulties and very great
anxiety. He had scarcely entered the field until
the clearest proofs of the divine favor were visible.
Hundreds resorted to his house to learn of the
great salvation of the Eternal God, and within
three months he seemed troubled about what was
usually a source of great joy. Multitudes coming

and almost as many turning away without relish for divine food and blessing.

His joy was mingled with grief and sorrow, grieved that better methods of doing the masses good were not at his disposal, sorry for the ignorance of a priest-ridden people.

Seed was taking root in the soil of earnest, inquiring hearts, divine light was springing up in some dark places, but with the appearance of the dawn of spiritual life was seen also the buddings of a fierce opposition, both from the priesthood and the government. His faith in God was strong, and slowly was he driven to the conclusion that the government would lift its arm against the Christ of Calvary.

Opposition from the priesthood was expected and Dr. Kincaid wrote, "the sooner the war begins, the sooner will Burma be saved." He longed to see the flame kindled that should purify the country of its abominations and idolatry.

Mrs. Kincaid lent a helping hand in the great and arduous work by her instructions in the school-room. And they had not toiled long together until sheaves began to ripen to the gleaner's hand.

The first convert baptized was a woman in

middle life.   Her conversion was evidently sound.
She said, it takes away my pride, and makes me
feel like a little child.   She desired baptism
because she said, "It is the appointed road for
those who worship God."

The scene of her baptism is described as one of
peculiar beauty and interest.

They knelt on the bank of the Irrawaddy and
lifted their hearts in prayer and thanksgiving for
those tokens of divine favor that permitted this
gathering, and Mah Nwa-Oo was buried beneath
the wave in obedience to the Savior's will.

How holy this spot.   How solemn and changed
the scene to anything witnessed there, where for
ages had echoed the song of the devotee.   How
cheering the display of Jesus' saving power and
love, where the walls of the Golden City flung
their shadows and the spire of the royal temple
gleamed over their heads, as at that rude altar of
prayer they offered to Heaven's King the first
fruits of the gospel gathered by Dr. Kincaid at the
capital of the Burman Empire.

Though heathens beheld and wondered, while
God was with them what need they fear?

"Be not afraid of those that kill the body, and

after that have no more that they can do."—Luke
xii, 4.   Not a breath but that of prayer, and the
words of the divine commission.   Well might they
take courage and hope for better days in Ava.

And God allowed not that hope to fail, for only
a few days later they gathered at the river again
and baptized Moung Kay, who only four months
previous had been acknowledged one of the most
popular preachers of Boodhism in the royal city.
Moung Kay first heard the gospel from Ko San-
lone, one of the native assistants of Dr. Kincaid.

Ko San-lone found Moung Kay explaining the
sacred Pali to a large body of venerable men, and
when opportunity offered, asked :

"Have you heard that there is a God Eternal,
Who is not and never was subject to any of the
infirmities of men?

"No."

"There is such a God, and His sacred word is in
Burma."

With what power these words fell on the ears of
this most popular preacher of Boodhism in the
royal city may be partially conceived by the out-
come.   Ko San-lone explained to him some of the
leading doctrines and designs of the Christian sys-

tem. His heart was pierced. He asked for a book,
and on the fifth day afterward threw away his beads,
forsook the pagodas, refused to bow to idols, and
made no offerings to the priests.

Having read the words that are spirit and life
and the power of God unto the salvation of believing souls, he was drawn by the power of the Holy
Spirit to behold Christ, the mediator between God
and man. He made a close personal search into
his own inner life, examined himself, and was
enabled to see things as never before, and acknowledged the possession of a new life in Christ—a new
heart—and said, "everything is new." He could
scarcely sleep or eat. His conversion and baptism
created no small stir in the city, and marked a new
era in Christian missions in Ava.

The claims of Christianity were more widely
felt, and its power exemplified in the few disciples
who owned Christ as their King.

Not the lowly alone, now, but men of distinction
and men in high places both sought and found the
truth, and joyfully testified of Christ's saving
power.

Dr. Kincaid, by request, now visited the Mekara
Prince, the most learned man in all Burma, to con-

verse on science and religion. At first he was most
attracted by scientific subjects, but soon he was
looking after the excellency of the knowledge of
Christ, and pronounced the Epistle to the Romans
"wonderful" beyond anything he had ever read.

He acknowledged the religion of Christ to be
pure and holy—different from and better than any
other. But the want of moral courage and faith
allowed him to remain where he was so far as a
public profession was concerned.

Fear and a spirit of cowardice kept many from
acting out the convictions of their hearts.

While Dr. Kincaid felt no doubt about the ulti-
mate triumph of the cause of Christ in Burma, he
had fierce opposition and bitter persecution and
trials to encounter. Surely none could rejoice
more than he at every advance step made by the
gospel.

The feverish and threatening attitude of the
government quickly passed, as clouds before the
summer sun. And God in love opened a wide and
effectual door for the gospel in the great and idolatrous capital of Burma.

By the close of the first year a little church had
been formed, and hundreds and thousands had

heard the gospel of Christ, and while few, comparatively, renounced the superstitions of Guadama,
many, it is thought, believed and silently accepted
the gospel, and may have greeted on the golden
shore at his approach, him who braved so many
dangers and offered so many earnest prayers in
behalf of benighted Burma, where he endured
hardships that but few men ever have been enabled
to endure, to give the gospel of peace to the priest-
ridden worshipers of false gods and idols made of
wood and stone, the workmanship of their own
hands.

CHAPTER IX.

SOWING SEED BESIDE FRESH WATERS.

"To preach the gospel in the regions beyond, and not to boast in another man's line of things made ready to our hands.—*2 Cor. x:16.*

> The man of God his message bore
> To those who never heard before,
> Of Jesus Christ, God's only son,
> Who for the lost so much had done ;
> And yet was willing more to do,
> To place redemption full in view
> Of those who long to know His love,
> And seek through Him bright homes above.
> The wild beast's lair and robber's den
> Both terrors to the bravest men
> Are broken up and check no more
> Salvation's flow on Burma's shore.

While Dr. Kincaid recognized the advantages of Ava, over every other city of Burma, for disseminating the gospel, and struggled hard to establish a church in the capital that should live forever, he also longed to explore that vast portion of the empire lying north of Ava, and into which no missionary had carried the gospel of peace.

From strangers who visited the capital he learned enough to impress him that this vast portion of

Burma was densely populated, rich in resources, and under the transforming power of the gospel and the touch of civilization, its wastes would be covered with happy Christian homes, whence streams of living light should flow and chase the darkness of pagan night into the eternal past, and the song of happy trusting pilgrims float on wind and wave from side to side and end to end of this empire of spiritual darkness.

Moved by such impulses, Dr. Kincaid planned a tour of exploration designed to reach to the very borders of China and the frontiers of Assam.

The brethren of the mission, seeing at a glance the magnitude and importance of such explorations as were contemplated, approved the bold endeavor. Only a little time was needed to put everything in readiness for the journey, but no sooner were all things ready than the government too was ready to warn Dr. Kincaid that he could not make such a tour of exploration. "This was more," they said, "than any foreigner ought reasonably to expect."

Hastening to the Thoot-dau, he found the spacious hall crowded with hundreds of people, and the ministers thronged with business. He squeezed and elbowed his way through the mass of spectators, secretaries and petty officials, until he stood fairly in the presence of the lords of the land, with the queen's brother at their head. He was asked:

"What does the American teacher want?"

Having planned a tour to Siam, with everything now ready for the journey, to-day a message from your lordships informs me you oppose my going by way of Bornea and Moyoung. I would learn the ground of your opposition.

"You must not go. We cannot consent to your going through our northern cities and giving books to the people. You can go by way of Bengal."

"That would take me a whole year."

Let it take eight years, the haughty nobleman replied.

"Being a religious teacher, I should be allowed to go where I choose."

"You must not go," was the only reply, and all efforts to learn the cause of their strong opposition availed nothing.

But Dr. Kincaid was not the man to be baffled or abandon an enterprise of such importance as this to the cause of missions, both at home and on the field. He longed to sow in the beautiful valleys of the Irrawaddy and other places the wonderful

words of life, that others coming after, might
see and gather the harvest that should ripen to
the reaper's hand.

He sought an interview with the queen's brother,
from whom he learned that the ministers were not
of one mind regarding the proposed tour. This
fact enabled him to go the more boldly to Moung
Yeet, an Atwen woon who was most persistent in
his opposition, who, after hearing a full statement
of the whole matter, said: "I have opposed your
design; but now I see it in a different light, and
will lay the matter before his majesty's officers."

After many delays and much anxiety, a permit
from the government was procured, and on January
27th, 1837, Dr. Kincaid embarked on what proved
not only to be an important but a perilous voyage.

Scenes of magnificence met their gaze on either
hand. The country passed through was one of
"uncommon beauty," but nothing worthy of
especial mention occurred until they had tied up
their boat for the night at the little village of Ya
tha-ya and found themselves at the very mouth of
a robber's den. Their arms for defense consisted
of one musket and two cavalry pistols. These were
put in readiness for an emergency. The threaten-

ing attitude and boisterous manner of the villagers
furnished a wakeful spirit to the occupants of the
boat, and while the head man gave positive orders
for all to keep away from the boat, the lawless
character and determined manner of some of the
men furnished occasion for a night of deep anxiety,
and the hailing of day dawn with relief and delight.
Moving up the river in the afternoon they met with
a very different company of people. This company
were elderly people, about twenty-five or thirty in
number. They were Shyans, male and female, and
each dressed in coarse, dark blue cotton. Whether
at work or not, they smoked from pipes with stems
three or four feet long. They had come from a
province about two hundred and fifty miles to the
north-east, and were on a pilgrimage to places of
reputed merit in various parts of the empire.

To the question, "Why do you take so long a
journey?" one, wrinkled with age, replied with
energy: "Our years are many, and we shall visit
all the most distinguished gods in the kingdom,
that we may get peace and merit before death."

Dr. Kincaid asked: "By worshiping the gods
of your country do you get peace?"

"Yes; and we have heard there are gods in

Amarapura, Ava and Pagan, and that under them there are relics of Guadama, which possess indescribable power. To visit these places and make offerings and pray is meritorious."

Dropping his pipe and looking Dr. Kincaid full in the face, with a deeply anxious expression, he added: "What do you think? Is it true?"

"No; it is all wrong. The gods you are going to see are made of brick and lime. They cannot see your offerings, hear your prayers, or help you. The true God, who made heaven and earth, made you and me, gave us power to speak and think, gives us the three seasons — the warm, cold and rainy—the Eternal God, whose presence, power and goodness are everywhere, that God is here, and hears all we say. He sees you and me, though with our bodily eyes we cannot see Him. He is holy, free from sin, never sick, never sees old age, and never dies. He is God—the true God—and beside him there is no God."

'Wonderful language,' 'extraordinary words,' replied a number with one breath, and eagerly wanted more. This company of venerable old people were out searching for the very blessings found in, and flowing through, the gospel Dr.

Kincaid was so ready to pour into every listening
ear. These earnest and devout people were ignorant of the Being who made them, yet distinctly
conscious of accountability to some supreme being.

At the village of Kyouk-man, where they stopped
for the night only, a few days later, Dr. Kincaid
spoke to the people by moonlight, and after distributing some tracts and copies of the scriptures,
and all were wrapped in slumber, Dr. Kincaid was
aroused by a low voice calling, 'Teacher, teacher';
and starting up, the man who had called began to
apologize for disturbing the teacher at such an
hour, and said on his return home a neighbor had
read about God to him from a tract, and learning
where the neighbor had procured such a treasure,
he came lest the morrow would find it too late.

The voice betokened a man of age, and coming
in the darkness, waist deep in water, betokened
commendable earnestness and zeal. A book and
some tracts were given, with some brief words
explaining the character of God, his purpose and
plan of redemption. The poor old man who heard
for the first time in his life of an Eternal God, who
purposed man's recovery from ruin, left, pouring
out a shower of gratitude.

Our next stop was in the beautiful town of Kyouk-kyih, the residence of the governor of the province of Monhein.

The governor received and entertained Dr. Kincaid in a most hospitable manner, and freely gave him much information concerning his people and the population of his province. His wife and other members of the family were very kind, and made the stay of American teacher as pleasant as possible. To the governor Dr. Kincaid gave two tracts, to his wife a New Testament. For them they seemed extremely grateful, and were free to converse on the subject of Christianity.

In a village still further up the river a large room was filled with attentive hearers, who listened until a late hour to the gospel of Jesus. They were orderly and attentive, and said they had never supposed before that there was any other religion in the world but their own worthy of consideration. But the idea of an *Eternal God* and of a way of escape from the punishments of hell, they deemed worthy of attention, and said they "must be considered."

Hearty receptions were given them at many towns, both on the Irrawaddy and the Mogaung rivers, the head man always providing a room for public service, and the people flocking in manifested the most respectful attention.

Finally, reaching Mogaung, the farthest north of any city in Burma, and situated about three hundred and fifty miles from Ava, Dr. Kincaid stood at the borders of a vast wilderness and in the shadows of the Himmeleh Mountains, separating Burma from Hindoostan, skirted by a territory crowded with people and abounding in mines of amber and serpentine stone. He made a thorough survey of the city and surrounding country, and gathered all possible information concerning the population and character of the people.

As Dr. Kincaid summed up the results of his survey and looked in every direction, and could not only see the great need of the people on every hand who groped their way in heathen blindness, but many willing and anxious to come to the light, need we wonder that he decided to return home, and place the knowledge gained by his tour before the churches in America, so that enlargement of plans and work should correspond with his enlarged views and hopes of the conquest in time of this mighty people for God.

Taking leave of the governor and his household, they soon were rapidly descending the river with faces homeward, full of hope and greatly encouraged with the results of their research, with no thought of the perils awaiting them. The obstacles to the enlightening and saving of the people of the empire were less formidable, and access to them much easier than hoped for. He said : "I may be too sanguine, too much inclined to look on the bright side, but after four years acquaintance with the government at Ava, and after traveling the whole length of the empire, visiting almost every city, town and village on the Irrawaddy, from the Martaban gulf to the Himmeleh Mountains, and forming an acquaintance with many of the provincial authorities, and knowing the character of many tribes of Burma, I have at least had opportunity of forming some idea of what can be done.

Only a few years previous to this it was not thought possible for a missionary to live in Ava; * * * preach the gospel, make disciples and baptize them into the church of Christ.

And I wonder whether all the Scotch *grit* and the divine grace of a Dr. Kincaid were not often needed in planting and holding the little church that only numbered twenty at the end of four years.

CHAPTER X.

CAPTURED BY ROBBERS.

"The Lord is my light and my salvation; whom shall I fear? The Lord is the strength of my life; of whom shall I be afraid? When the wicked, even mine enemies and my foes, came upon me to eat up my flesh, they stumbled and fell. Though an host should encamp against me my heart shall not fear."—*Psalm xxvii, 1-3.*

The perils and privations which Dr. Kincaid underwent on his passage down the Irrawaddy from Mogaung, form a thrilling chapter in his eventful life. Burma was in arms. The horrors of anarchy and civil war had quickly spread over the empire upon Thur-ra-wa-di's revolution (an account of which may be found in Chapter XVII.) Large bodies of armed men were rapidly organized into prowling and marauding bands, whose occupation was plundering and burning both cities and villages, and rendering all travel exceedingly hazardous. Having completed his explorations and surveys so far as his resources would permit, Dr. Kincaid turned his face homeward, and with little hindrance rapidly passed the one hundred and fifty miles of picturesque country from Mogaung, the most northern city of Burma, to the little village of cruel bandits that awaited the coming of anything on which they might fall as prey.

On the morning of February 27th, 1837, a small boat with twelve men in it was seen hurriedly approaching them. One of the servants was ordered to hold up a Burman musket, to show that they had government protection. At sight of the musket the robbers wheeled and rowed away with all haste, and the hope that all trouble was over was no solace long, as the robbers were seen coming again, with a second boat of twelve more well armed men, all carrying with them muskets and long spears, and each having a Burman sword hung over his shoulder. Dr. Kincaid now stood up with two loaded pistols, and warned them to be off or suffer the consequences, and although they immediately rowed away, it was for reinforcements. Dr. Kincaid encouraged his men to ply their oars and escape if possible, but soon six boats, with seventy or eighty men, with furious yells came down upon them, apparently bent on their destruction. They formed themselves into a crescent, and at the distance of two hundred yards or more, fired a round of twenty-five or thirty shots at Dr. Kincaid and his boat. His men had fallen down into the bottom of the boat. The balls whistled about him uncomfortably near. Some went over his head, some on either side, some into the water, but no one was harmed. Realizing that it was madness to longer resist such a force single-handed, Dr. Kincaid threw up his hands and told them: "Come and take all I have. Don't shoot any more, for you have nothing to fear. No further resistance will be made." Notwithstanding all he said and his full surrender, they loaded and fired several more shots at him, but through a merciful providence no harm was done to a single one on board. And while Dr. Kincaid remonstrated with them for firing upon a single and empty-handed foreigner, they closed in upon him with fixed bayonets, spears poised in the air, and swords drawn, as if they fully purposed cutting him into a thousand pieces. A dozen swords were over his head, and his whole body was encased in the steel points of swords, and bayonets, and spears, so it was impossible to move in any direction without coming in contact with these sharp weapons of war. These savage monsters roared, grinned, threatened, and uttered the most horrible imprecations. On reaching the shore his books, papers, maps, medicines, provisions and money were laid in a general heap, to be divided as spoils among his cruel captors, who also took all his clothing except shirt and pants. He told them he would not be thus treated, but they must take him before their chief man. An armed guard of several men was placed over him, and he was ordered to lie down while the robbers divided their plunder. Dr. Kincaid says: "Nor could I keep from smiling to see the ludicrous appearance that many of these wretched men presented. One had on a shirt, another a jacket, and another a pair of pantaloons."

Many boats had been robbed within the past few days, twenty-nine on the same day of Dr. Kincaid's capture. They were gathering plunder and spoil at a rapid rate, but they seemed most concerned about what disposition should be made of their foreign prisoner. They were under great excitement and the indications were that he should be disposed of in the way least liable to make them future trouble.

Their custom was to destroy such prisoners as would make them trouble in case of escape.

While conscious of this fact, Dr. Kincaid says, "I felt that the superintending providence of God had faithfully preserved my life amidst scenes and dangers quite as fearful as the ones in which I was now involved, and I had a faint hope that I should be preserved."

In these trying circumstances I lifted my heart to God in prayer for his continued protection. At the breathing of this prayer one said, "I will kill him." Another said, "I will cut his head off."

The chief was a dignified man, noble in his appearance, possessed of an open and benevolent countenance, and possessed perfect control over his men. He betrayed momentary sympathy for Dr. Kincaid's condition more than once and having the fullest confidence and respect of his men, the captive was encouraged to ask some favors which were promptly granted. He says, "I put my hand on the knee of the chief, and represented to him my destitute condition and exposure to the sun by day and the damp and chilly dew by night. My jackets and pantaloons being restored without a murmur, I was encouraged to ask the further favor of a cloak of coarse cloth that would make me comfortable while asleep at night."

"A man of most desperate appearance, with villiany and cold-blooded murder stamped in his face, sat upon my cloak, and when the chief asked him to restore it to me he drew it still closer under him, as if to hide it, but I pointed it out, and the chief ordered him to give it to me."

The fellow, cursing, took it from under him, and discovering it to be of greater value than he at first supposed it to be, muttered dissatisfaction, again placed it under him, and drew his sword with the apparent determination not to give up his share of the spoils without a struggle. Several of his wild comrades rallied around him. "I was not, however, to be deterred from my purpose with these threats, and again called the attention of the chief to my cloak."

He turned his head away as I spoke, which was the signal of dissatisfaction, and in a moment a hundred swords were drawn, and with dreadful imprecations and yells they rushed toward me in great passion, as if to destroy me. This was enough. I saw that further entreaty would be in vain, and that I had incurred the displeasure and created the dissatisfaction of the chief by my earnest and repeated applications for his clemency and favor. There appeared at once to be great confusion among the robbers, who were walking about in great fury. "Soon," says Dr. Kincaid, "I was ordered to the boat under a strong guard, and was informed by one of my boatmen that the robbers were sitting in council, to determine whether to kill or to release me."

It was a state of considerable anxiety and suspense to me, and I was relieved only to make uncertainty certain, for when the council broke up the youngest of my Burman boys, a lad about sixteen, approached me in tears, and told me that the robbers had decided to behead me at sundown, the time of day when all Burman executions took place. The knowledge of my sentence was almost more than I could bear. For a few minutes I was completely overpowered. A cold perspiration came over me; my breathing was short and interrupted; my mouth became parched, and my tongue seemed to cleave to the roof of my mouth. It was not the fear of death, but the character of my death. I looked on the dreadful place in which I was called to die, and the nature of the circumstances by which I was surrounded—alone, among a band of fierce robbers, outlaws and murderers; their cold-blooded determination to take my life without a single exciting cause for convicting me; no friend to communicate with, and to tell the state of my mind; none, perhaps, to carry the tidings of my death to Ava, to the mission and my family—for it was very doubtful then whether any of the Burmans who were with me would ever escape. The sensations were dreadful, and I can scarcely bear, even now, to think of them.

However, I recovered in a very few minutes from this state of mental despondency, and thought, what is this? It is nervousness; it will never do; I must·rally. If this is death, I must meet it with Christian firmness. I am still in the hands of my Heavenly Father, who has oftentimes preserved me, and why need I fear what men can do unto me; they can kill the body but they cannot destroy the soul. I know I must die, and if this is the time and the manner which God has appointed for my departure, I do resign myself into His Almighty hands, and I trust, come what may, it will all be for His glory. Thus I struggled with my feelings, and reasoned with myself, until I gained the mastery, and until entire composure and reconciliation to my fate had settled over my senses.

I had nothing now to do but to await the time fixed for my execution, and the hour drew near. But man appoints and God disappoints. I watched the fleeting moments as they sped by, and I could not keep my eyes off my executioners, who appeared to be engaged in an angry war of words. They became louder and louder, and I found, by catching a word now and then, that they were divided in opinions as to my sentence of death.

A faint hope stole over me that the hand of God was about to be extended for my preservation, and I uttered a prayer for relief. The robbers drew their swords, looked fierce, and seemed ready to plunge them into each other, so violent was their anger. In a little while they were on their way to plunder a village a few miles away, and by the hour set for my execution not a man of the banditti was on the ground.

As I remember to have heard Dr. Kincaid relate this providential escape, it was about in this wise: The robbers had some fears as to future results, and they reversed the decision to behead him at sundown, but there was such anger and excitement that nothing seemed to appease their anger until some one proposed the sacking of the village, and the motion carried so unanimously that they went like a flock of sheep where the leader had jumped the fence into new pasture, and not one stayed to look after the prisoners, who, after getting some rice, took their boat, put into the current, and were soon out of sight of the scene of their trials and fears, and gave God the deepest gratitude of hearts rejoicing over escape from such a fearful death.

CHAPTER XI.

IN GREATER PERILS, YET PRESERVED.

"Thy God whom thou servest continually, He will deliver thee.—*Dan. vi, 16.*

Some bandits led to the chief robber's place,
A captive so full of womanly grace,
Her very deportment ennobling to see,
An honor to woman wherever she be.

These bandits so cruel were after her gold,
And whipped her quite hard to make her unfold
The place of concealment that held it secure;
In dignified nobleness she stood there, demure.

With womanly form subjected to pains,
Her hair fast clotting with blood from her veins;
No mortal but bandit, with heart like a stone,
Could quicken the blows at each dying groan.

At last all was over, and death was complete.
Her first-born fell with the babe at her feet,
Cried, "Mother! don't die and leave us alone!"
No answer came back, not even a groan.

One robber kicked as he would a dog,
The eldest of seven 'till she lay as a log,
Unconscious of baby now left to her care,
Or whether of seven one child he would spare.

And not a word of kindness was spoken,
Save by a captive whose bonds were unbroken;
Nor aught of help could this captive afford,
But on that bandit worm epithets poured.

Escaping that night from this robber clan,
A perilous journey on foot he began;
Over mountain and vale, through jungle and glen,
In ways never pressed by the footsteps of men.

After escaping the perils and threatened death related in the preceding chapter, nothing interrupted their passage or security until just at day dawn when they came in sight of the village of Sabanago, about one mile ahead. It was soon evident that they should meet no friendly reception at this village as their ears began to be pierced with the most terrific yells and a number of armed boats were seen to put off from the shore to head them off as they came on down the stream.

There were about two hundred of the furious men who quickly surrounded Dr. Kincaid's boat which was instantly boarded by four well-armed young men, who seized on their prey like young tigers; they took hold of Dr. Kincaid's neck-stock and dragged in every direction so furiously that he was choked near to insensibility. In this state and perhaps with a death-struggle, he threw up his arms and released himself from their grasp. This but made them more furious. They seized him again and tore off his neck-stock, jacket, shirt, pantaloons, and shoes, leaving him without a vestige of clothing. Recovering from the shock of this cruel treatment, he stood erect before his fierce and brutal captors, who at once began tying his arms after the manner of securing Burmese criminals. Dr. Kincaid determined to resist this treatment, and told them they should not tie him, that he never had been tied, and that he should resist being tied until death. With this they set up a loud laugh and grinned awfully at him but did not persist in tying him.

When they reached the shore, they dragged him along some yards from the place of landing, and there made a ring in the sand around where he stood and told him for his life's sake not to step beyond it.

A guard of armed robbers, numbering from fifteen to twenty, surrounded this ring, and thus left him scarcely any chance for escape.

One of his Burmans, who saw and felt for his exposed condition, took off his waist-cloth, tore it in two, and handed Dr. Kincaid one-half of it, which he secured around his waist, and in this dreadfully exposed condition, without an article of food or drink except what he begged from the women of the village, as they passed and re-passed

down to the river for water, did he remain six days
and six nights, without any shelter from the
scorching heat of the midday sun, or the cold,
damp air of night.   And besides this, he did not
know what would be his fate from day to day, or
from hour to hour.   He was continually harrassed
by impertinent questions, and the cowardly threats
of his cruel tormenters, who left no means unem-
ployed to make his situation as miserable as
possible.

During the time that Dr. Kincaid was imprisoned here, his four boatmen and three of his boys
made their escape in the night.   The fourth and
last one, Tha-oung by name, came to him on the
third day, and observing him casting his longing
eyes in the direction of Ava, Dr. Kincaid knew
that he wished to inform him of his intention to
run away.

He walked all around Dr. Kincaid at a distance,
and then came nearer, as if desiring to speak to
him.   His manner also showed an unwillingness
to leave his teacher alone to die at the hands of the
cruel robbers.   At last making his way to him he
sat down by his side and wept like a child, telling
him that he intended to make his escape that

night; that the others had run away, and to escape
was his only show for liberty.

Dr. Kincaid told him to go, and if he ever
reached Ava and the mission station to give all the
information concerning him that he could.

After some words of Christian counsel given to
the boy by Dr. Kincaid, and the assurance that if
he would remain true to his profession they might
hope to meet again, the boy, with almost a broken
heart, took leave of the fettered prisoner. He
only went a short distance, however, when his
mind was made up to return, and arriving, he said:
"*Teacher, I will never leave you, but will stay by
you until I die.*" Dr. Kincaid endeavored to dis-
suade him from keeping this resolution, but to no
purpose. His mind was made up to remain a prisoner.

On the very next day, however, this faithful boy
was selected from among the prisoners to go into
the interior as the servant of one of the petty chiefs
and a number of the gang. Nothing more was
heard of him until two or three months afterwards,
when he returned to Ava. Dr. Kincaid now
thought very seriously of attempting to escape,
but it was a very hazardous undertaking. He was

about two hundred miles from Ava, and should he escape, must avoid the river and take his chances of finding a pass over the mountains, where possibly human foot had never gone before. Hour by hour he watched the mountain's side, to see if he could possibly discover a pathway or hope of relief from his present peril.

The perils across the mountain way he could not fully know. Those surrounding him were exceedingly grave and threatening, so his mind was made up to escape, and being entirely destitute of clothing, and feeling sadly the effects of his constant exposure, he endeavored to single out that man of all his guard whose countenance displayed the greatest amount of benevolence, determined to make advances, and if possible obtain his favor. Having selected his man, he spoke to him, and reasoned with him about his exposure, telling him how unaccustomed he was to go without clothing, and to sleep without covering at night. In this way he soon won upon him so that he went and brought him an old piece of sail-cloth, and afterwards the pantaloons of which they had stripped him when first taken prisoner. Dr. Kincaid feared to ask more lest suspicion should be

aroused, but determined to go on his perilous journey the first opportunity that offered itself for
escaping.

During the six days that Dr. Kincaid was detained
among these robbers, parties were sent off every day
to plunder travelers and to plunder in the neighboring towns, and often, in the night, the sky was
lighted up by the flames from burning villages.
These parties, after robbing and burning the houses
and barns, would drive into their haunt large herds
of cattle, and roast them, and feast and drink and
smoke all day.

Dr. Kincaid was imprisoned not more than
twelve feet from where the robber chieftain sat,
and from morning until night parties of the banditti
were bringing in women and children, and the
chief would examine them to learn where their
valuable were buried, it being the custom of these
people to hide their gold and jewels in jars in the
earth, for fear of fire and thieves.   If these women
refused to tell him where their valuables were buried,
they were shamefully treated and cruelly beaten.
They would strip them, throw them on the ground,
tie their hands and feet together, and then, with
large rattans, a robber would scourge these females

in a most unmerciful manner. Sometimes, even
if they would yield from their intense sufferings,
and tell where their gold was hid, they would go
on beating them because the robbers would say
that was not all.

Many of these women, though their sufferings
were dreadful, bore the scourging with astonishing
fortitude. It was not the purpose of the robbers
to put them to death, but to torture them ; and
after whipping them until their backs were torn
and lacerated, they would take their spears and
pierce holes in their bodies half an inch in depth,
and after making thirty or forty of these stabs,
they would take pieces of split bamboo, and dip
one end in melted sulphur and stick the other end
into the punctures made in the bodies of these poor
captive women, and then light them as tapers, and
in this they seemed to take great delight.

Dr. Kincaid was obliged to witness these horrid
cruelties, for, although he would close his eyes, he
could not close his ears to their lamentations, and
the cries of their children, who had to look on and
behold these monsters beating and abusing their
mothers.

On the sixth day he witnessed a scene of cruelty

far surpassing all others. It was the scourging of a female who had with her seven children.

She was taller than most Burmese women, of slender frame, and had a fine, intellectual countenance. With a dignified nobleness, she stood before her captors, and with an expression of defiance, refused to answer their questions. Dr. Kincaid looked upon her and her seven children clinging around her, with the deepest interest.

She was beaten by a robber, a thick, muscular man, who could strike with great power. The chieftain would cry out, "Strike quick." Then the blows would fall faster and with more vengeance. Her hair fell down over her bare back, and was soon heavily clotted with blood, and her face cut unmercifully. Every blow Dr. Kincaid expected would be the last. Finally her head fell on her shoulder, her eyes were fixed, her lips pale, she rolled over on the ground. Death had done its work.

Her eldest child, a beautiful girl, who had held the infant in her arms, and her five brothers and sisters wept bitterly, when they found their mother was dead. This girl laid the babe at her feet, and fell down upon the body of her mother, uttering the most piteous and piercing cries of anguish, repeating again and again, "Mother, don't die and leave us."   ·

Dr. Kincaid looked on those fiends in human shape and waited to see if there was one there to speak a kind word to these orphaned children, but among them all there was no one to pity. Instead, one of them violently kicked the poor child, to get out of the way, and she fell over speechless on the ground. This brutality was too much to bear; a maddening sensation filled him with wrath so that he arose to avenge the cruelties no longer bearable but found himself tied and unable to get hold of the cruel monster, on whom he poured every epithet that human language could invent, wholly indifferent as to what might be his fate. To tantalize him the whole band burst into a loud laugh.

His mind was settled at once to escape at all hazards. The remainder of the day he kept a close watch on his guard and on the mountains. Night came and the guard as usual took it in turn to sleep. But it was no time for him to sleep, as failure to escape and the hope of success were in the balance, and the chances against hope, and if hope failed his life must pay the forfeit.

To insure the success of his purpose, he amused the guard with entertaining stories about America, the steamboat and the steam engine, until a late hour, and long after midnight, while the guards all slept, as he hoped they would, he crept away in almost breathless silence, beyond the guard, to where he could quicken his steps, and soon reached the skirts of the forest.

Once in the jungle, he breathed more freely, and thanked God for the possibility of putting himself beyond the reach of his cruel captors before morning. At sunset he reached the mountains, much exhausted, and with anxiety, loss of sleep, hunger and the fatigue of travel, he felt it impossible to take another step, and after returning thanks to God for his great deliverance, and asking His protection on his journey, he rested and slept. When next he awoke the sun was near meridian, and, starting up, he hurried as fast as possible on his way, through a dense and tangled forest, which never had before, perhaps, been trodden by the footsteps of man.

He traveled all day without water, but at sundown came to a little ravine, which was followed until a muddled spring was discovered, holding, possibly, three quarts of water, with a dark red-colored scum more than half an inch thick covering the surface. It was not a time to be over-particular. So, after partaking of his remaining stock of rice, he laid himself down, pushed the scum away, and drank until his burning and raging thirst was entirely quenched.

Without rising, he rolled over and passed the night in peaceful slumber until the sun shone full in his face. Stiff in every limb, and with feet bleeding and blistered, he set out again on his journey.

He found it a heavy task to urge himself forward at the slow gait he was compelled to travel. More than once frail nature was ready to yield, but when he would stop and think, here I am to die in the deep recesses of a mountain forest, where human beings seldom, if ever, travel, far from home and friends, with no eye to see but the eye of God. The idea of so awful a death preyed upon him, so he was driven to renewed efforts, again and again, to reach some human habitation. At last, turning the crest of a mountain, he could travel with more ease, and finally came in sight of a village, which he rightly judged to be a village of robbers. He knew the robber chief always lived in the largest house, and made his way straight to the largest house, and to his great joy found the robbers were absent. He kindly spoke to the chieftain's wife, and told her his story of sorrow. The woman said, 'And have you a mother?' Yes, I have a mother in America. And Dr. Kincaid has often said, 'My own mother could not have been kinder to me than was this woman. The big tears rolled down her cheeks as she witnessed the evidences of cruelty to the escaping, inoffensive sufferer. After a hasty meal and some directions as to how he could avoid the robbers, they parted, the woman deploring the work of her husband and people and Dr. Kincaid rejoicing at a kindness which he cherished to the very close of his life.

Late in the evening he came in sight of the hamlet of a Burmese peasant; reaching the cottage he made known his situation. A man venerable with years invited him into his house, his wife set before him a large dish of cold boiled rice. After enjoying this most welcome reception, he soon fell asleep on a mat and peacefully slept until the

following morning when his journey was again
resumed, and after an uneventful day of weary
travel he reached a spring as the sun was throwing
his farewell evening shadows onto the curtain of
night. He quenched his thirst and lay down to
await an opportunity of asking food from some
passerby. Soon he saw a woman coming with her
jar for water. As she approached Dr. Kincaid
spoke kindly to her bidding her not to fear, and
told her his condition was due to his capture by
robbers from whom he had escaped and was trying
to make his way home to the capital. She
directed him to remain where he was, that there
were many robbers in the country and should
he enter the village suspicion would be created.

Filling her jar she went to the village and soon
returned with a meal of boiled rice. Returning
thanks to God, he partook of his solitary meal,
and again lay down and slept undisturbed till
morning, when he found it quite difficult to make
progress owing to stiffness in his limbs and the
soreness of his feet.

The day was nearing its close without any
remarkable event or change to break the monotony
of the lonely way, when turning the brow of a hill

he came suddenly upon a group of bandits, eating their evening meal. They were horrid in appearance, and coming so unexpectedly upon them caused some alarm, but he walked boldly on with seeming indifference. They looked at him with a fiendish grin, but no one seemed willing to leave his meal to molest the weary and jaded traveler. Losing no time even to look back, he was soon out of sight, and fell on his knees to thank God for another deliverance. After another night's rest he pursued his way through a sparsely settled country, and here and there would find a cleared patch of ground tilled by some poor natives, who would hide themselves as he passed, as if afraid of the sight of man.

Till now he had gone eastward toward the Shan country, but circling back at last, came near a little village on the Irrawaddy, about thirty-five miles above Ava.

He avoided the village, but found the watering place on the river where the jars were filled by the women. He laid himself down in the sand, hungry and exhausted with travel, and waited the coming of the Burmese women to get water, remembering that he had *never* been refused food asked for at the hand of a Burmese woman.

It was not long until he obtained boiled rice from two native women, and laid him down and slept once more.

Awakening, he started at once on his way, and soon met a face he had seen before, who, on promise of an exorbitant price, undertook to deliver him at the capital.

On his arrival home, exposed as he had been by nakedness, hunger, privations, hardships and travel, he was so changed in appearance that his wife, whom he had parted with only about three months before, did not recognize him. But soon the hand of love was binding up his bleeding and blistered feet. The four natives, who had mourned for Dr. Kincaid as dead, came in a few weeks later, having suffered many privations and tortures between their first escape and arrival in Ava, where they rejoiced with great joy to find living, though not yet well, him they had mourned as dead.

CHAPTER XII.

THE COUNTRY AND CUSTOMS.

While this tour of exploration was regarded by all the missionaries as very important, it was also regarded as very hazardous.

Many of the river villages were then robber nests or dens, the vocations of whose people was to prey on other villages and the boats that passed up or down the river.

To make such a tour by land was next to an impossible undertaking, as up to this time no provisions were made either by the general government or by the local authorities to make roads or build bridges.

It was a very rare thing in Burma to meet with anything that would in America be called a road.

The only roads in the empire were those leading into the larger towns and cities.

If a loaded ox could pick his way and get over ten miles a day the road was regarded as good.

Ferries were kept on some of the larger streams,

the smaller ones the missionaries might wade
or employ natives to carry them over.

The soil was very rich and fertile, capable
of yielding the most bountiful harvests, but the
oppressed and indolent people, with their rude
implements and very limited knowledge of agri-
culture, got only a tithe of the possible harvests
from these fertile valleys.

They kept large herds of red cattle, but in most
villages cows were never milked, and as the Burman religion forbids the slaughter of cattle, their
use was quite limited.   They were used in plough-
ing sometimes, and as pack animals and to draw
carts.   Horses were never used for any other purpose than riding, were never harnessed or worked,
hence were not regarded as of the same value
they are to many other countries. ·Fowls were
very abundant and grown mainly for fighting purposes, a cruel sport of which the natives were
found to be passionately fond.   The men would
gather themselves into groups under the shade of
the large trees in the heat of the day and greatly
enjoyed themselves watching the movements of
these feathered warriors.

Women were very rarely, if ever, seen about

such places. They were much more industrious than the men and were generally employed in some way to profit.

At Katha, once a city of note, located on a beautiful rolling plat of ground on the west bank of the river, a most beautiful valley, of very productive soil, stretches for miles to the east and south, dotted here and there with villages. To the north and west the country is irregular and rough.

February 12th, 1837, they stopped at a village on an island in the river. It was about sixty feet from the water up to the crest of the island, which was covered and shaded with most noble tamarind and palm trees. The local situation was most pleasant. The view from the island of these surroundings was grand.

Pushing forward at early dawn, before noon they were compelled by a driving storm to lay by and warm. The natives were very kind, and cheerfully built fires for the half naked and benumbed boatmen. Here Dr. Kincaid met some traders from the north, from whom he obtained some valuable information. These traders were Ka Khyens, no doubt a branch of the great Karen family. "They have no object of worship, no rites, no priesthood, and yet had some idea of a supreme being.''

They had a tradition that they once possessed books, but lost them. ''They had no tradition of ever having a king, or ever being consolidated in an empire. Their government was patriarchal.'' They had been oppressed by the Shyans, Burmans and Chinese, the only governments of which they · had any knowledge. Their traditions are all handed down in song, in which all join, from the oldest to the youngest. The dead are not burned, but buried with becoming solemnity. They are an agricultural people, growing rice, cotton, tobacco and maize, or Indian corn, but recently introduced in the country, which they eat in the milk.

The females spin and weave and dye their own cloth, and assist in cultivating the land. They never intermarry with other people.

They regarded the Burmans as their natural enemies, by whom they have been taxed and oppressed to the very last point of endurance. Wars have been frequent and determined, and woe to the Burmans or Shyans who have dared to follow these

Ka Khyens into the fastnesses of their own mountain homes.

This visit of Dr. Kincaid through the northern
part of the Burman Empire was the first attempt
to carry the gospel into those unexplored portions
of the empire north of the capital, and was vastly
more important than conceived by many. Although his stay was very brief and his work quite
limited among the multitudes in the northern half
of the empire, himself robbed and his life jeopar-
dized and threatened, both by the men whom he
went to bless, and the wild beasts whose lair he
must pass in fleeing from the murderous outlaws
and bands of robbers who sought to render escape
impossible.

Those who look on the development of missions
in later years will readily admit, I think, that this
visit brief, hazardous and unpromising as it at
first seemed to be, was the entering wedge to open
the northern half of that great empire to the gospel. It was no "fool's errand," no "fruitless
mission;" but was the dawning of a new era.
That visit carried the first rays of light and life
into many homes and hearts in half that vast em-

pire, over which the great curtain of heathenism hung heavy and low.

And while comparatively few heard of Jesus or his great salvation from the missionary's own lips, enough was heard to start the inquiry among the Ka Khyens and Karens as to whether the strange white teacher, in his visit, did not at least begin the fulfillment of that very ancient tradition among them that "*some time a messenger will come* and restore the book our carelessness permitted a dog to carry away and destroy."

This country abounded with plenty, and was regarded by Dr. Kincaid as the easiest place for a mere living of any country he ever visited. The lakes and streams were bountifully supplied with choice varieties of fish, and fowls were very abundant.

On excursions often made through the country, they were compelled to sleep on bamboo platforms, made on top of four posts stood in the ground, perhaps eight by ten feet square, and eighteen or twenty feet high, which they ascended by means of a rope ladder that was drawn up after, to prevent reptiles and wild beasts from becoming too familiar. Wild beasts were frequently encountered,

but Dr. Kincaid was fortunate in never being personally attacked.

I would be glad to pursue this descriptive chapter further, but hasten to record in the next some
of the conditions attending Dr. Kincaid's arrival
at home, together with the sad state of the whole
country because of the revolution that placed
Prince Thur-ra-wa-di on the throne of the Burman empire.

CHAPTER XIII.

REACHING HOME — THE REVOLUTION — CHANGING FIELDS.

Blistered and bleeding and scorched with the sun,
At last his perilous journey was done;
His wife thought a stranger approaching the door,
Nor had she e'er seen such a stranger before.

A native or foreigner, who can it be ?
That seems like one familiar to me.
Ah ! relic of manhood—thou joy of my life !
What has made thee unknown to thy wife ?

Spared art thou yet, thanks be to God;
But why has fallen so heavy the rod?
"Calm down, dear wife, and bind up each wound,
Whence my blood has marked each step on the ground."

Poor mortal, what suffering, and why must it be ?
Have wild beasts or bandits had fast hold on thee ?
"In perils with both, and more than one band,
Yet God hath delivered with His loving hand."

On his arrival home from his perilous journey, March 11th, Dr. Kincaid found the city full of distressing alarms. Prince Thur-ra-wa-di had risen against and dethroned his brother, and the whole country presented heartrending scenes and desolation. The empire was laid waste, half the population had been robbed, and war was raging in all the distant provinces. The capital and neighboring cities had also been invested with his armies, and so great was the danger that threatened the mission families that, for a few days, they took shelter under the roof of Colonel Burney, the English resident. During the continuance of the war and after the new king had ascended the throne, sanguine hopes were cherished that the prospects of the mission would become more encouraging. The character of the prince seemed to warrant such expectations. He had always sought for intercourse with foreigners, and had been remarkable for the liberality of his opinions.

He had expressed his disapproval of the exclusive jealous policy of the government, and often had he spoken against the annoyance given the missionaries, especially the vexatious manner of the government's treatment of Dr. Kincaid. But hope was doomed to a sad disappointment, as within sixty days the new king had expressed himself averse to the American teachers, and that he should order a discontinuance of their labors. As he was a very learned man and stood high in Burma, and had shown special kindness as a prince to Dr. Kin-

caid, there was great significance in the report of
such a stand being taken against the missionaries.
So Dr. Kincaid at once sought an interview with
the king. The king received him with evident
marks of kindness, and declared that he was not,
personally, unfriendly towards him. "But, now
being king of Burma, he was *tha-tha-na-da-ya-ka*
(defender of the faith), and must support the religion
of the country, and said to Dr. Kincaid, 'You must
give no more of Christ's books.'

This was said in the presence of the whole
assembled court, and implied that the royal will
must not be trifled with.

Thus surrounded, and with almost absolute cer-
tainty of a war between the British government
and the new king, it was deemed best to leave the
capital, at least for a time.

On June 17th, Dr. Kincaid withdrew from Ava,
after a residence of about four years, in which time
he had learned and suffered much. But while the
capital afforded opportunity of meeting people from
all parts of the empire, and sending the gospel by
single copies out into a thousand channels, twenty-
seven members were left in the church at Ava.
When Dr. Kincaid arrived at Rangoon, July 6th,

he found the missionaries already gone to Maulmain in consequence of the threatened revolution,
and the decrees of the viceroy against them.
Hastening on to Mergui by way of Maulmain and
Tavoy, he made this his temporary home, while
visiting and preaching at points of interest in the
adjacent country, and wherever he went blessings
attended his efforts.

In a village twenty-five miles from Mergui the
people eagerly listened to the word of life, and a
congregation of about one hundred joined in the
worship with interest. Visible results attended
every visit to this place, and it was his privilege to
administer the Lord's supper here to a church numbering thirty-six happy converts.

About one hundred and fifty miles south of
Mergui and thirty miles from the Tenasserim
coast, Dr. Kincaid visited among the islands,
where he found a people in the most abject poverty and degradation. The islands were densely
wooded and of nearly every size and form, some
are low and level, others mountainous, with wild
and craggy shores. The climate is so delightfully
pleasant, one instinctively exclaims, What a beautiful world! A thousand green islands and islets,

gorgeous with the beauty of nature and dense with life.

Here Dr. Kincaid found a people free from all religion. They had no God, no temple, no priest, no liturgy, no holy day, no prayers. Of God and immortality they had never heard. They were free from all conventional rules in their domestic habits. They had no houses, no gardens, no cultivated fields, no domestic animals, except dogs. He says, "Such abject poverty and such degradation, such entire destitution of all the comforts of life I never saw. I have been five days among them teaching them the knowledge of God." "I have resorted to every method of instruction, in order to reach their understanding; with what success is known only to God." Two evenings many of them remained until a late hour; on the last evening Dr. Kincaid urged them to pray now to the Eternal God, of whom they had now heard, and repeated for them three or four short prayers, when by their urgent request he taught them one of three or four sentences and then asked them if they would forsake all sin and serve the great God who made heaven and earth, when some eighty or one hundred immediately replied, "I will, I will."

He then told them about the Karens, their conversion and learning to read. They unitedly urged Dr. Kincaid to come and live with them on their islands, promising that they would all learn to read and become Christians.

His passage over the Tenasserm Mountains was full of interest. After a six hours' march he arrived at the foot of the mountains and put up for the night. Here he found two families living in solitude, and to his great joy among them he found four persons whom he had baptized. They gave him a most cordial welcome, spread a mat on the veranda, brought water for washing and drinking, dressed a fowl for his dinner, and did everything that kindness and Christian courtesy could dictate.

While but four in these two families had been baptized, no less than sixteen of them were believers in Christ, and gave credible evidence of a change of heart.

Leaving these Christian friends, Dr. Kincaid started on his toilsome journey over the mountains, not in destitution, fleeing from the merciless robbers, but hastening to fill the destitute with the word of life. He says:

"We set off in Indian file, for more than three

hours wending our way along the bed of a mountain stream, sometimes only two or three feet deep.
On either side the mountains rose up to a great
height."

In many places the stream was filled with brush
and fallen trees, over which they had to climb
where practicable, but often they were obliged to
creep on their hands and feet for fifteen or twenty
feet together.

After reaching the head of this stream they
ascended a high range of mountains, which
stretches along from north to south between the
Tenasserim and the ocean.

From exhaustion Dr. Kincaid was obliged to lie
down and rest a number of times before the top of
the mountain was reached.

The mountains they found to be irregular, precipitous, and covered with a dense forest. They
traveled for about four hours amidst these wild and
rugged mountains, often having no other path than
that made by wild elephants and tigers.

This was their own undisputed territory, and if
one may judge from the evidences on every hand,
must conclude they are quite numerous. Mon-
keys, too, in countless numbers, ranged the forests

of this, their native home.   There are several families of these, some quite large, without tails, and
the Karens tell us they are very bold and savage,
often attacking travelers, if but one or two are
found together.   When great numbers join in encouraging an attack, they engage in deafening
yells, and the only security against them is in setting fire.   They, like other wild animals, are
afraid of fire.

Mountain storms are terrific, yet full of grandeur.
For nearly two weeks the weather had been suffo-
cating, with thunder storms every evening.   Some
times the roll of the thunder is so continuous and
loud it is difficult to make one hear only a few feet
away.

About 4 o'clock in the afternoon the clouds began
to gather in dense, black masses, and as the Karens
told them storms were much more severe in the
mountains than on the plains below, they halted
for the night, and began to provide what shelter
they could against the gathering storm, rapidly
approaching them.   Dr. Kincaid was too much exhausted to do more than give some directions.   In
less than an hour a comfortable shelter was ·pro-
vided, and before their meal was ready the storm

was upon them, and with one or two possible ex-
ceptions, this was the most terrific they had ever
witnessed. The whole atmosphere appeared to be
a living mass of fire. There was a continued roar
of thunder, mingled, almost every breath, with
sharp, deafening peals, like the discharge of heavy
artillery. The rain, too, was poured out in torrents. The awful grandeur of the scene, however,
banished all thought of inconvenience and dis-
comfort.

Time passed unnoted, hours seemed but minutes;
and there was neither room for levity nor sadness.
The huge masses of clouds, hurrying on, rolled up
and down the sides of the lofty and rugged mountains. The blazing atmosphere, the incessant roll
of thunder, and the torrents of rain, accompanied
with strong gales of wind, altogether formed a
scene most impressively sublime.

The next morning two of the company were
suffering with fever. One, a fine young fellow,
after two or three efforts, sank to the ground, unable
to walk. Dr. Kincaid had fever during the night,
but was well in the morning, and set out at an
early hour, and reached the Tenasserim that day
in the afternoon, about one hundred and forty or

one hundred and fifty miles above Mergui. They passed that day through some of the wildest scenery of nature, most of the way without the slightest evidence that any human being had been there before them. Dr. Kincaid says: "I suppose we walked half the distance in the channel of a stream, having, some part of the way, a most welcome sandy bottom, with only a few inches of water; then again rocky and precipitous, with occasional deep basins, taking us near to the chin in water.

Tracks of the rhinoceros, elephant, tiger, deer, wild hog, and monkey were everywhere seen. Their hard beaten and frequent paths give one an idea of their fearful numbers.

There was no spot of barren earth to be seen. Vegetation in wild luxuriance grew everywhere, So one could scarcely check the desire to see civilization impart its magic touch to that fertile soil, and utilize its wasted force.

The Tenasserim is not so long or large as many of the rivers in Burma or Siam, but at this place is about one hundred yards wide.

The chief who had visited Dr. Kincaid at Mergui two or three times, had been expecting his

arrival for some weeks.   He had built a zayat, in
which himself and neighbors met on the Sabbath
to worship the Christian's God.   In the five houses
in this small hamlet were thirty-two or thirty-three
souls.   Two or three miles distant were other hamlets, where the people were sitting in the shades of
death—enemies to, or wholly ignorant of God.

At early lamp-lighting all came to hear the gospel.   The first text used there was: ''And as
Moses lifted up the serpent in the wilderness, even
so must the Son of Man be lifted up.''

The next day was the Sabbath, and messengers
were dispatched to other hamlets to notify them of
the arrival of the American teacher, and invite
them to come and hear the gospel.   A part of the
day was spent in examining the candidates for baptism.   A second sermon was preached at half past
ten in the morning, after which the examination
of candidates was resumed, and four persons baptized in the Tenasserim about 4 o'clock in the
afternoon.

After commending the little church to the care
of God, and promising to send them a teacher, if
possible, he turned reluctantly away from that little bethel.

Visiting two other hamlets, and preaching Christ to the people, they put up for the night on a sand-bank, not daring to fasten to the shore on account of tigers. Only two days before a Karen had been seized and carried off, though seven or eight men were with him, and made every effort to save him. The whole country is wild and mountainous, and covered with heavy forests.

Every day found Dr. Kincaid active in visiting hamlet and village and hut and home, preaching to a people whom he regarded as the "good ground" spoken of by the Master, while the Burmans fitly represented the "wayside."

Some miles distant he visited the greatest Karen chief in his province. This chief had a large house, and, for a Karen, was wealthy. He soon learned who the American teacher was, and affected great indifference to his message; put on haughty airs; said Christ's religion was turning the heads of his people, and hinted that he was not so insane as to forsake the old paths trodden for ages by his fathers. He spoke Burman fluently and correctly, which was no small attainment for a Karen, as they can never pronounce a word that ends with a consonant.

Dr. Kincaid commended him for adopting new sentiments with extreme caution, and never without clear evidence of their truth; then added, ''Your fathers were more enlightened than mine, for they knew the name of Jehovah, and in every age they rejected idolatry. I preach to you now the Jehovah of your fathers and offer you instruction from the book which he has given.'' Not allowing him to reply, Dr. Kincaid proceeded to read several passages from the New Testament, and appealed to his own apprehension of truth, if these things did not commend themselves to his conscience.

His airs were gone; and with altered tone he acknowledged that he often thought the religion of Christ true.

He said, some months since, he had a child very ill, and made offerings to the Nats, but his child died. He made a solemn promise then that he would never make such offerings again; but said he had tried to give up drinking spirits and could not, and so could not be a disciple of Christ. He was urged to believe in Christ as the only way to obtain eternal life. He was urgent with entreaties that the missionary return again.

And though every kindness was shown him, and the fields were whitening rapidly to the reaper's hand, Dr. Kincaid longed to return to the capital, where the multitudes jostle together, in the hope that the fierce opposition might be broken down, and the forces wasted in evil might be utilized for the glory of God and the spread of his gospel.

So in the autumn of 1838 he supplied his place at Mergui and hastened to Maulmain, hoping to proceed at once to the royal city, but finding it injudicious to proceed further just then, he sent two of the native disciples, Moung Na Gua and Moung Tha Oung, to visit the church at Ava. It was only a short time until he received the following letter from one who had remained at the capital.

MY BELOVED TEACHER, KINCAID:—After reaching Ava and finding my parents, I lost no time till I found out the residence of all the disciples. Some of them have removed to Amarapura, and they are so scattered that they do not meet oftener than once a month, some once in two months. Soon after getting to Ava I wrote a letter, and on desiring to take it to the English residents, the Burman

officers forbade me, saying, 'There was no permission to go or to send letters.   Besides this, a priest
went merely to see the English, and was seized and
taken away to execution, so that I did not dare to
send you a letter.

Now, feeling a great desire to write to you, I
have gone secretly to a foreign merchant, and he
will send the letter.   After this I hope to be able
to send you letters often.   Not long after getting
to Ava, Ma-ee, the daughter of Ko-shwa-nee, died.
After this, Moung-moung died of fever, and was
only ill three days.

The disciples here are like sheep without a shepherd, and are anxiously looking for the time when
the teachers can come.   I wish much to return to
you, teacher, but my father and mother are old and
very infirm, and cannot get about well, so that I
must remain and support them by my labor.   When
the disciples meet, they consult together about
fleeing from this city to Maulmain, but as yet dare
not make the attempt.   The disciples remain
strong in the faith of Christ, and pray to God
continually.   The writer, Ko-shwa-nee, is perse-
veringly preaching the gospel.

New-dong-gee and Moung-you come to Ko-shwa-
nee's house every three or four days, and reason
with him about the law of God.

To the beloved teacher, from

MOUNG-OO-DOUNG.

CHAPTER XIV.

A GRACIOUS WORK IN ARRACAN.

"He shall come down like rain upon the mown grass; as showers that water the earth. They that are in the wilderness shall bow before him.—*Psalm lxii, 6-9.*

Writing from Maulmain January 20th, 1840, Dr. Kincaid gave his reasons for going to Arracan, prominent among which was that no real missionary work could be done where he was. Like the merchants, they could have staid in their houses and held the fields, if this were all to be done. There was no difficulty about living in Burma. But they could not teach, as the people dare not go near the missionaries. Another field opened "The command was plain. 'If they persecute you in one city, flee to another.' Paul at one time was forbidden of the Spirit to preach the word in Asia; nor was he supposed to go into Bithynia, because, in the divine arrangement, he must first preach the gospel to a people made ready in Macedonia."

Results justify the inference that God called Dr. Kincaid at the time out of Burma into Arracan.

Locating at Akyab he zealously prosecuted his work, and soon was permitted to see most wonderful displays of God's peace.

He wrote May 4th, 1840: "I preach three times on the Sabbath in my own house, and four times during the week at three different places in town. My hearers vary in number from twenty-two to over one hundred, while from five to twenty come to the house every day. The heat is rarely below 90°, and much of the time is 95° to 97° in the coolest place about the house. My two native assistants are all I could wish. They labor hard to win souls to Christ. From one hundred to two hundred persons hear the gospel daily. Many dispute with an ingenuity and earnestness well calculated to put to shame the 'idle and ease-loving ministers of Christ.' It is often truly affecting to see the deep workings of the Spirit, and the anxiety in mustering arguments to sustain that religion revered and trusted by them for many generations past. All false religions walk together in fellowship, but the uncompromising claims of the gospel, when they do not compel respect and attention, awaken the most bitter opposition. The heathen are accustomed to respect all religions, because they regard them as adapted to the various circumstances and wants of different nations.''

They are often pleased, therefore, with the gospel at first; but when they come to understand its fearful denunciations against idolatry and all unrighteousness of men, that it pronounces the whole world in a state of apostacy from God, that all men without faith are without God, without hope and must perish forever; and that the gospel is the only system of truth, and the only refuge for the whole race of man, they either become patient hearers or bitter opposers, and sometimes take refuge in infidelity.

Among frequent callers was one of peculiar sentiment and high position, who had been titled by the king of Ava M' ha-don. He had a contemplative turn of mind, and ''one day, on. the occasion of a baptism, this learned and venerable man was at the water and joined in the singing of two hymns, and afterwards paid the utmost attention to all that was said and done. When the converts came out of the water, in answer to the question some one put to him, he replied, in an earnest and elevated voice, 'This is the true religion, and I must be baptized and be a disciple of

Christ.' His constant attendance at worship created a great sensation all over the city. The priests had a meeting to inquire into the cause of his extraordinary conduct, and to them in the most frank and open manner he said, 'I have found the true religion after worshiping idols and pagodas for more than ninety years.'

"About this time Dr. Kincaid was greatly encouraged by the intelligence that reached him of the wonderful triumph of the gospel among the Karens of Bassien Province." An occasion for "great rejoicing had its beginning in the latter part of 1837, and its influence continued to spread from village to village until converts were counted by thousands. Moung-Shway-Moung, who was baptized late in 1835, was appointed by the king governor of all the Karens in the Bassien Province. He was sent down from Ava in the latter part of 1837. The Karens soon found he was a disciple of Christ, and that he would shield them to the utmost of his power from oppression and persecution.

The Karens said "He was a just man and would never take bribes; that on the Sabbath he closed up his house and remained alone."

About this time a celebrated young chief was converted. "He possessed great energy and a powerful intellect, and all his influence was thrown into the work of publishing the knowledge of God among his countrymen. This revival was an extraordinary display of divine grace. Probably two thousand souls were turned from worshiping demons to the service and worship of the true and living God. This, too, under the reign of a jealous and intolerant king." "It was God's glorious work."

In the early spring of 1841 the lamented Comstock, with his family, visited Akyab and during his stay of sixteen days, joined Dr. Kincaid in an interesting preaching excursion. They visited a number of villages and the town of Arracan. Here they preached to large and solemn assemblies, both in private houses and in the open air.

Some reviled, but the great mass honestly acknowledged they were in the dark and knew no way of escape from the pains and punishments of hell. Said one, "I have lived seventy years, and have labored to keep the five great commands, and have found no peace." Said another, "The power and glory of our religion have long been waning and must entirely vanish." Such sentiments were common among the people. "Some of the villagers who received tracts and heard the gospel during the excursion, soon afterwards came to Akyab, and were able to repeat much of what they had heard. They also read the '*wonderful words*" and came for more."

Among the interesting inquirers, came one "of much intelligence who confided in his own wisdom and his ability to defend his old religion, who was driven to yield one point after another, until confronted by "the miraculous birth and deity of Christ," which he regarded as a fable appended to the Christian religion; but his mind was not at rest, his conscience was stirred. One day Dr. Kincaid read and explained for hours the first chapter of Hebrews. The next day he said to Ko-Bike that he read and prayed nearly all night and felt very unhappy, for he thought he should not live long and must go to hell." He remained in this state of mind several days when he came with joyous countenance and said he had obtained peace. "Now I know," said he, "what it is to believe in Christ, for I have the evidence within

my heart.'' Another inquirer of the city of
Akyab is especially worthy of mention. He was
a man possessed of great wealth, and had for some
time been arranging to build a large Kyoung
(monastery) and had already spent many hundred
rupees, when he first heard the gospel. He
was so affected by the truth as to dismiss his work-
men till he should examine fully the claims of the
new religion.

Preaching is often interrupted by the heathen
for the purpose of asking questions, and after
preaching for about thirty minutes one warm night,
in a moonlight so clear Dr. Kincaid could read by
it without difficulty, questions poured in so upon
him it was impossible for him to proceed. On one
occasion, when he had closed the book, one man
strongly defended Gaudama, and a discussion of
nearly two hours ensued, during which one who
had been a strong opposer of the new religion
threw in valuable words of testimony. At last my
''adversary forsook the field of argument and began
to ridicule and revile'' his fellow as a heretic, saying: ''You have become a disciple of the cross,
have you? You join with this foreign teacher, do
you? to prove that our god is *no* god, and that our

religion, which has stood for a ·thousand years, is only a cheat and a fable. Who will carry you to your grave when you die? Your father and mother will despise you, and your brothers and sisters will shun you as they would a leper." "You are like a dog that is coaxed away by a thief—you may as well lick honey from the edge of a razor as to listen to this foreigner." "Very well," replied my ally, "I have reviled this religion and this teacher more than you have, but I was a fool with both eyes shut; his religion is true, and everybody would" own and accept and love "it if they knew what it is. We make a god of wood, put a rope around his neck, then carry him to his own place, put a fence around him, and leave him till the white ants eat him up. We would not serve a thief so bad as this. There is as much proof that Gaudama was a monkey as that he was a god." At this some turned away with their fingers in their ears, while many listened to the very last, eleven o'clock at night.

Perhaps the most interesting occurrence in connection with Dr. Kincaid's stay at Akyab was the visit of Chetza, the mountain chief. Their first interview was in May, 1841. Early in July follow-

ing the chief sent Dr. Kincaid an important letter,
revealing traditions of their people for ages past,
concerning a *good book* God had once given to their
fathers, and through their carelessness had been
carried away by a dog and destroyed. This incurred
the divine displeasure against them. They could
now neither read nor write, but were anxious to
know the true God, and to be taught the true book.
They had looked for the coming of a messenger
with a book of light and knowledge, hence were
quite open to receive the missionary and the Bible,
at least to find out whether their traditions and
hopes were filled in Dr. Kincaid's visit to them.

The letter · bore the name Chetza, the great
mountain chief, with the names of thirteen petty
chiefs, stating:

"Our sons and our daughters we will deliver
over to you to be taught if you will have compassion on us." Following was a list of two hundred
and seventy-three names of boys and girls, whom
they wished to place under their care and instruction.

Dr. Kincaid wrote: "There is something
singular and interesting in this request. From
time immemorial they have held intercourse with

the Burmans, but have resisted idolatry. They have looked with apathy, if not with contempt, upon the imposing ceremonies of Budhism, its temples and pagodas, monasteries, idols, shaven-headed priests, its ten thousand burning tapers, its prostrations, its beads, its celebrated shrines, and pilgrimages." Like the Karens in Tenasserim and in Burma, they looked for a "*good book*," which would tell them of the true God.

Who can doubt the overruling providence of God in preserving these people from the idolatry about them, and the sending of his word to them in answer to the call, "Come over and help us."

CHAPTER XV.

"The dwellers in the caves and on the rocks
Shout to each other, and the mountain tops,
From distant mountains catch the flying joy."

Near the close of the year 1841 Dr. Kincaid perfected arrangements for a visit to the mountains. Chetza, fearing disappointment, made another visit to Akyab, urging Dr. Kincaid to come at once and teach his people the true religion.

Accompanied by Rev. L. Stilson for this purpose, a most interesting tour was undertaken December 29th. Their journey and reception among that remarkable people is replete with interest near to fascination.

They crossed the spacious harbor and entered the Ko-la-dan, a broad and noble river which has its sources in the Yuma Mountains, far to the north.

After ascending the Ko-la-dan between seventy and eighty miles, we left the Burman population and entered the Kemmee country. The change in

scenery was not less striking than the change in
the character, habits and manners of the people.
For the last seventy miles before it empties its
waters into the Akyab harbor, the Ko-la-dan flows
through a tract of level plain, dotted with villages
in every direction. Rice fields extend often as far
as the eye can reach. The monotony is well
broken by here and there dark, tangled forests.
Neither fences nor hedges were employed to protect
the great and wide-spreading fields.

The soil is exceedingly rich, and capable of pro-
ducing heavy yields of such plants, vegetables and
fruits as are adapted to that climate.

Thirty miles from the sea shore the land is
slightly elevated, and the mountains begin to
appear in the distance.

Leaving the plains, so full of small creeks
and rank growths as to be a laboratory of most
deadly fevers, we leave the Burman population,
and first come to low ranges of hills but constantly
ascending until the great tangled forests crown the
mountain summits. The winding river is broad,
deep and beautiful and its general course from
north to south.

As they were anxious to reach the home of the

chief, they visited but one of the many Kemmee villages along the river.

The landing was all that indicated we were approaching a village, as the timber came down to the water's edge, and some boatmen were cooking their morning meal. Climbing up a steep bank, they found a path that led to a village of near twenty houses, surrounded by a neat and well-constructed stockade. "The gate being open, we went in but saw no human being. After standing a few minutes in order to give no unnecessary alarm, and admiring the peculiar structure of their great houses, the neat and orderly manner in which they were placed, that is, in two rows, so as to have a broad street run through the center, we passed on and finally went out at the gate on the opposite end of the village and found ourselves standing on the bank of a noisy little brook, an object of great interest to us, as it was the first of the kind we had seen in Arracan."

"We saw pigs, goats and fowls in abundance and began to wonder where the inhabitants could be, as we saw none and heard no human voice."

"We suspected that the women and children had fled to the jungles when they had learned of the landing of strange-looking foreigners and that the men were probably in the rice fields, as it was about ten o'clock A. M.

While examining some peculiar trees that grew on the margin of the brook, a female with a child slung on her back rose out of grass only a few feet from us.

She appeared to be paralyzed with fear, and the poor child dared not look up. We were sorry our appearance should be more terrifying than the midnight growl of the most ferocious beast of prey.

And we assured her again and again that she had nothing to fear, which she evidently believed as she quietly returned to the village. Soon the men began to come in and then the women and children from their concealment, each woman with a child on her back and many with from three to six following. The men came and sat down by us, while the women remained at a distance or went to their dwellings.

Some of the men could understand Burman, and a few spoke it fairly well.

We stated that our visit was in obedience to the command of God, to visit all nations and instruct

them in his holy word. Such news proved interesting to them, and they were quite ready to receive
books that would enable them to look into and
understand these things."

"We left this interesting, cleanly little village,
and the next morning came to the mouth of the
river Moe, a fine stream fifty or sixty yards wide,
flowing from the north-east. About six miles up
this stream we came to the village where resides
the mountain chief. This beautiful village is situated on a fine elevation about one hundred feet
above the water level, in a great bend of the river,
and commands a beautiful prospect in this wild and
picturesque country. Three other villages are in
sight, while a fourth is not a mile distant. The
country was in perfect contrast here with all they
had seen for seventy miles above Akyab.

Lofty hills and deep valleys are here thrown
together in the utmost confusion.

Both hills and valleys are covered with tall forest trees, interspersed with bamboos, various kinds
of creepers, and in places grass ten to twelve feet
high."

For eight or ten months the chief had been
urgent in his requests for a visit, and the establish-

ment of schools among his people. It was therefore
to be expected that a hearty reception awaited Dr.
Kincaid and the Rev. Mr. Stilson, and things
should be made ready to their hands.

The forethought and care of the chief, however,
surpassed the most sanguine expectations of the
missionaries.

A new, well constructed and commodious zayat,
about fifty feet above the water level, had been
provided with pleasant walks and veranda. But
their surprise was greatest to find all ready for
their use two very neat bamboo bedsteads, surrounded with curtains. The chief must have seen
a bedstead in the mission house at Akyab.

The building, bedstead, and every provision
made had been done within two days' time.

When the chief discovered that the missionaries
had a small folding table and two chairs with them,
he was relieved of considerable anxiety, as he had
much anxiety about these articles, without any
idea as to how they might be constructed. The
chief was very kind, and exceedingly desirous
about their comfort.

The zayat was about fifty yards outside of the
stockade, and delightfully situated. When once

arranged in their new quarters, they were taken to
the home of the mountain chief.   The house itself
would indicate it to be the dwelling of some great
man.

The floor was five or six feet from the ground.
Crossing a large open veranda they entered in front
the great hall of audience.   It was a magnificent
room, and from the north afforded a most delightful view of the country in its native grandeur.   On
the left of the great veranda was a very large apartment, and on the right was a smaller one.   These
belong to the females and children.

His nine wives were all busy at work except one.
Some were cleaning cotton, some spinning, some
weaving, some cooking.   Each had a child slung
on her back, regardless of the kind of work that
occupied her, and each one seemed cheerful.   The
wife who seemed to preside over all, or to have
preference with her husband, was a dignified
woman of no ordinary rank—graceful; and she
impressed one both in appearance and manners
that nobility was innate, and not merely the result
of position.   Her countenance was intelligent, her
temper mild and amiable.   She impressed one with
the spirit of contentment and happiness.   Her

knowledge of the Burmese language was not
extended, but she betrayed no signs of ignorance.
Order and neatness prevailed, so as to make that
one an exceptional home. Indeed, the whole village was constructed in an orderly way, with a
view to the comfort of its people, and showed a
neatness, regularity and order so seldom met, it
was a pleasant luxury. The Kemmee's villages
and houses showed that more attention was paid to
the arranging for the comfort of the people than
with any people yet visited. The clothing was
scanty and peculiar.

The men wear turbans, and a four-inch belt
around the hips and between the legs; the females
an upper jacket without sleeves, and a lower gar-
ment, reaching from the hips half way down to the
knees.

It is remarkable that a people of such neatness
and care in the construction of houses and villages
should be so sparing in raiment. They have ample
supplies of material.

God had preserved these people from idolatry and
kept alive among them the tradition that the Supreme Being had given their fathers a *good book*,
which, through their carelessness, had been

destroyed by a dog, but which, in time, would be restored to them, and that they should then become a wise and happy people.

Dr. Kincaid, or Rev. L. Stilson, preached the gospel to these people every evening, in the plainest and simplest manner possible, but only a few understood the Burman language sufficiently to gain much information.

Those who understood believed, and expressed the opinion that all the Kemmees would accept the gospel when they could understand it.

With the exception of short intervals, from morning till night, efforts were made to gather words and sentences that would enable them to better understand each other. These people were quite numerous, as they occupied the valley of this great river Koladan and its tributaries, for a distance of two hundred miles, and were one of the greatest branches of the Karen family.   .

The Khyies inhabited the hill country and the great ranges of Yuma Mountains to the north, as the Kemmees do at the south.   From a line eighty miles north of Ava, all the hill country for more than three hundred miles, was inhabited by a people, Dr. Kincaid says, ‘‘I found, in all respects,

like the Karens," and were known as Ka-khyiens.
The Karens, Kemmees, Khyiens and Ka-Khyiens
were evidently but so many branches of the one
great family, formerly the sole occupants of that
vast country, but had been gradually driven back
by the Burmans from the valley of the Irrawaddy
and from the sea coast.

When Dr. Kincaid informed the mountain chief
and some of his people of their purpose to study
their language and provide books that would give
them knowledge of the true God, he said this decision gave him more joy than would the reception
of thousands in gold and silver, for, said he, "the
gold and silver would 'soon be expended," and
neither his children or people be any better for it,
"but if we have the knowledge of God we shall
die in peace." Could the multitudes who have an
unholy greed for gain decide as wisely as he, how
many more happy lives would render the dying
easy and make heaven brighter and better for their
presence there.

The village selected as headquarters for the .
Kemmee mission was beautiful and healthy, not
too far from the interior, and yet far enough to be

the center of a number of villages, embracing three thousand or more inhabitants.

No foreigner had ever been north on the river, past the boundaries of Arracan. The Burmese were afraid to penetrate the country, and it was quite difficult to get reliable information concerning much of that vast country. The Kemmees reported two powerful bodies of people far to the north, Lung-khe and Tsien-du, who differed somewhat from themselves in language. Beyond this little could be learned.

The Kemmees understood how to make an intoxicant from rice, which they used on great occasions. They regarded evil spirits as the cause of disease and many calamities, and on some occasions offered to these propitiatory sacrifices.

While they believed in a Supreme Being, the immortality of the soul, future rewards and punishments, they had no religious service.

They regarded theft, falsehood, adultery and murder as great crimes. They were proverbially a people of *one word*.

Do not suppose from the above statement that the Kemmees were a harmless and unwarlike people. Feuds were frequent, and difficulties rarely adjusted in an amicable way.

They harbored revenge, and sought opportunity to fall on their foes at a time when least expected to do so. They openly declared hostile intentions.

The conquering party would kill as many men as possible, and seize and carry away the women and children for slaves.

War did not seem a natural element of the Kemmees, but rather a circumstance—outgrowth of being driven back like the American Indians, until war seemed a last resort.

The introduction of books and schools among them laid the foundation for their civilization and happiness, for that people who gain a knowledge of "Whom to know aright is life eternal," must be prosperous and happy in this world, and happy in the assurance that it will be infinitely better in the beyond where we shall see Him as He is, and be like Him.

Their language was reduced to writing, books furnished, many hopeful converts baptized, among whom was Paiting, son of the mountain chief, a most devout and pious young man, whose constant prayer was, "O Lord, send a teacher from America for the Kemmees.

CHAPTER XVI.

A VISIT HOME.

" For not he that commendeth himself is approved,
but whom the Lord commendeth "—*2 Cor. x, 18.*

Let the " Hero " return to his home once more
   And arouse the people from shore to shore
To double their diligence and on to the fight,
   To crush out the wrong and build up the right.

Brother, thrice welcome to thine own native soil,
   And respite from labor or change in thy toil.
Be quickened our zeal by the news thou shalt bring,
   Of conquest for Jesus, Redeemer and King.

The courage that urged through jungle and glen
   As fleeing from bandits, or seeking *lost* men,
Make bolder our hearts to strengthen such hands,
   Till Jesus shall reign King over all lands.

For more than twelve years Dr. Kincaid had been ever busy on the foreign field, except as hindered by robbers and war. The health of his wife demanded a change of climate and in 1843 he returned to his native land accompanied by his wife.

He met with such a reception as proved that he was held in high esteem in the churches and homes of America.

But he found a sad lack of missionary zeal, in many of the churches both north and south. And that same love for the lost that led him over mountain and plain, through jungle and glade, to carry the gospel to the millions then wrapped in the curtains of night, led him to travel through almost every state in the Union making such thrilling appeals for the heathen as to awaken everywhere a new and marvelous interest in behalf of foreign missions. To narrate the striking incidents connected with the visit and his untiring efforts to produce a missionary conviction everywhere, furnish thought for a thrilling chapter. But as this is all fresh in the memory of many living witnesses, we only notice a few points of special interest to profit the generations that were not stirred by his thrilling appeals. A very imperfect idea of their effect as they fell from his own lips can be portrayed through the pen. To appreciate these appeals, place before you a form well developed, in full prime, all aglow with the subject under consideration, every fibre of his frame wrought to a high tension with deepest emotional feelings, pouring forth in every strain, his whole being stirred to that intensity under which it is impossible to remain unmoved.

Never, while memory lasts, could a hearer forget the impression made as he recounted the parting scene of the lamented Comstocks with their children, and the last words that Mr. Comstock uttered to Dr. Kincaid.

"Owing to the difficulty of educating them in a heathen land, the children were entrusted to the care of Dr. Kincaid to bring to America."

While together at the Comstock's one day word came that the ship was ready to sail, and that they must prepare at once to embark.

On the arrival of this expected messenger, Mrs. Comstock arose, took a child in each hand, and walked with them toward a grove of tamarind trees near the house. After walking a little distance, she paused a moment, looked at each of her children with all a mother's love, and imprinted an affectionate kiss on the brow of each. She then raised her eyes to heaven, silently invoked a blessing on their heads, returned to the house, and delivering her children into his hands, and said: "Brother Kincaid, *this I do for my Savior.*"

Brother Comstock then took his two children by the hand and led them from the house toward the ship, while that tender mother gazed upon them, as they walked away, *for the last time.* She saw them no more on earth.

Reaching the ship, about two miles off in the bay, "we descended to the cabin. When Brother Comstock entered one of the staterooms with his children; there he knelt with them in prayer, laid his hands on their heads and bestowed a father's blessing on them, tears all the while streaming down his cheeks. This affecting duty over, he resumed at once his usual calmness." He took leave of Dr. Kincaid with a gentle pressure of the hand, and, with upturned face still bedewed with tears, exclaimed as the boat moved away, *"Remember, Brother Kincaid, six men for Arracan!"*

This proved to be their last meeting and parting on earth. The very day their children were safe at Sandy Hook, April 28th, 1843, the mother's spirit, released from earth, returned to God who gave it; and three days less than a year later, Brother Comstock followed her to rest. And while peacefully they sleep side by side in the graveyard at Ramree, under the tamarind trees, may their devotion be emulated by many who shall read, *"This I do for my Savior."*

As he stood before a large assembly with his

12

soul on fire, encouraged by the conquest manifest in tears and half-smothered sobs, hear him once more call upon his audience to remember the parting words of the beloved Comstock, as he asked, "Shall I return to that heathen land without 'Six men for Arracan?'"

It was this illustration of Christian heroism, so touchingly related, that called from the pen of Charles Thurber the following beautiful lines:

"Six Men for Arracan.

" The mother stamped a burning kiss
   Upon each little brow ;
So dear a sacrifice as this
   She never made till now.
Go, go, my babes, the Sabbath bell
   Will greet you o'er the sea;
I'll bid my idol ones farewell,
   For thee, my God, for thee.
But off they'd gone, those little ones,
   I saw them gaily trip,
And chatter on in merry tones,
   To see the gallant ship.
The stricken sire, he'd often drank
   Sad draughts at duty's beck,
He leads them calmly o'er the plank
   And stands upon the deck;
As pale as polished Parian stones,
   As white as Arctic snows,
Beside those young and cherished ones,
   The stricken father bows.
He breathes one prayer, he prints one kiss

And turns him toward the shore.
He felt, till now, the babes were his,
   But they were his no more;
The silken tie more strong than death,
   That bound their hearts was riven,
And floating on an angel's breath,
   Rose up and clung to heaven.

Why lingers he upon the shore ?
   Why turns he to the deck ?
Perhaps to say farewell, once more,
   Perhaps one look to take.
O no, but calm as angels now,
   That kneel before the throne,
When twice ten thousand thousand bow,
   And say, "Thy will be done,"
He said, " My brother, when you stand
   Beyond the raging deep,
In that delightful, happy land,
   Where all our fathers sleep,
When you shall hear their Sabbath bell
   Call out their happy throng,
And hear the organ's solemn swell,
   And Zion's sacred songs,
Tell them a herald, far away,
   Where midnight broods o'er man,
Bade ye the solemn message say,
   " Six men for Arracan."

While in that happy land of theirs,
   They feast on blessings given,
And genial suns on healthful airs,
   Come speeding fresh from heaven ;
Tell them, that, near yon idol dome
   There dwells a lonely man,
Who bade ye take this message home,
   " *Six men for Arracan.*"

Sweet home, ah, yes, I know how sweet,

Within my country, thou,
I've known what heartfelt pleasures meet,
  I've felt, and feel them now.
Well, in those lively scenes of bliss,
  Where childhood's joys began,
I'd have ye, brother, tell them this,
  " Six men for Arracan."

O when the saint lies down to die,
  And friendship 'round him stands,
And faith directs his tearless eyes
  To fairer, happier lands;
How calm he bids poor earth adieu,
  With all most dear below.
The spirit sees sweet home in view,
  And plumes her wings to go;
Stop, dying saint, O linger yet,
  And cast one thought on man;
Be this the last that thou forget
  "Six men for Arracan !"

At a gathering held in the large round house of
the Sansom street church, when Dr. Williams had
read a report on the duty of churches in reference
to the cause of missions, Dr. Kincaid rose to move
its adoption, and said: "There are a great many
intelligent people who question whether, in this
day, we are to expect the same success as marked
the history of the primitive Christians in their
efforts to furnish the heathen with the gospel."

But if it be preached "in all its length and

breadth and richness, with like spirit, there will be like success."

He was fully convinced that if the gospel were preached in all its simplicity, stripped of all its human adornments, it must ever prove to be the power of God to believing men in every land in every age.

There were but three missionaries in Burma in 1830, two of whom were qualified to preach. These were reinforced so that in 1843 seven or eight were preaching and doing much other work to spread the gospel among the perishing.

The translation of the scripture into different tongues was going on. Tracts were published and freely distributed, and while the government was unfriendly and even threatening, such an amount of the leaven of God's grace had found its way into the hearts of the people as to lift all Burma on the wings of prayer towards the mercy seat, where the windows of heaven were confidently expected to open, and showers of blessing flow to every thirsty soul.

True, the missionaries complained of a lack of faith and that fullness of the divine presence that always gives zest and power to the gospel. Their realization of this lack put the apostolic prayer in their mouths, "Lord, increase our faith," and the power was given in due time, and he who was in perils among robbers and wild beasts lived to see the time when he could travel from end to end and side to side of the Burman empire, and every day save one dine in a Christian home, and every night but one lodge with a Christian family.

CHAPTER XVII.

BARRIERS BREAKING AWAY.

"Whom he would he set up, and whom he would he put down."—*Dan v. 19.*

The chief cause of Dr. Kincaid's prolonged visit in this country was the distracted state of the Burman Empire. After the accession of Thur-ra-wa-di to the the throne, whose arbitrary policy was the immediate cause of Dr. Kincaid's leaving Ava, the condition of the country for a long time was such as to render it impossible to occupy it as a field of labor with any hope of extended usefulness.

But, beside the contracted views of the government, so unsettled was the whole state of their political affairs that it was impossible to calculate what would be developed in the future. The missionaries could, therefore, but await the unfoldings of providence.

Soon events transpired which awakened confident hopes that the day was near when that dark land would again be thrown open to missionary labors.

Dr. Kincaid wrote, "The king of Burma is dethroned, and an entire revolution has taken place in the government. Prince Mekara is made regent, and the Woon-gee who signed the Yandabo treaty is associated with him in the new administration. This change of government will be hailed with rapture through all the provinces in the empire, No two men could be more unlike than the Mekara prince and the deposed monarch. The one by nature a tyrant, and the other amiable and unambitious. I became acquainted with both these princes in 1833, and from both received great kindness. Thur-ra-wa-di manifested no interest in any conversation but such as related to the power, wealth and political influence of nations. He pretended to admire France, Persia and China, and never concealed his dislike of the English.

No one could be with him long without perceiving that his hatred for the English arose from his dread of their power. He took a daily paper from Calcutta, had it translated, and when he could fix on any reverse or disaster, it seemed to afford him the highest gratification.

He was five feet four inches high and well formed. His forehead was remarkably high and retreating, and his eyes brilliant and piercing.

When pleased, his eyes were peculiarly fascinating; but when angry, they were lighted up with dreadful vengeance.

The Mekara prince was somewhat taller, but less muscular, and had a high, full forehead, with large, intelligent, smiling eyes. When thoughtful and studious, there was a slight tinge of melancholy in his countenance, but in conversation there was a glow of kindliness spread over his whole face. His inquiries always turned upon religion, science and literature.

The philosophy of religion, or the great principles brought out and inculcated by different systems of religion, interested him deeply. Next, mathematics, astronomy and languages interested him. He was the most learned Burman in the world. To gratify his thirst for learning, he procured Rees' Cyclopedia and other works, a pair of large English globes, and a telescope, in which he could see the rings of Saturn and the satellites of Jupiter.

"I gave him a copy of the Bible, and a copy

of Galladet on the Soul, in the Burman language.
Paul's Epistles to the Romans interested him more
than any other book.   He often spoke of its pro-
found reasoning, and of the great principles there
brought out.   Dr. Price had taught him to read
English, but he was not able to speak it.

At his request, Dr. Price commenced an English
and Burman dictionary, and after his death it was
taken up and completed by Mr. Lane, an English
merchant, and printed at the expense of the East
India Company.

The amiable and humane character of the Mekara prince was proverbial in Burma.

Ko-gway, a venerable old man, who became a
Christian, and afterwards deacon of the church in
Ava, told me he was an eye-witness of a successful
act of the Mekara prince in behalf of two state
criminals.

The men were leaders in a rebellion in one of the
frontier provinces.   They were brought to Ava
and sentenced to be crucified.   This sentence was
carried into execution without the walls of Ava, a
little after sundown.   The next morning, very
early, the prince, then about twelve years old, went

out with his attendants, and passed near where
these two men were crucified.

Hearing their agonizing cries, he inquired what
it meant, and being informed, he directed his
attendants to hasten with him to the palace.   He
threw himself at his father's feet, and with bitter
tears, implored him to have mercy on the men.   The
king gave orders instantly to have the men taken
down.   It was a little after sunrise when they
reached the place, and their groans had become
feeble, as life was fast ebbing away.   The wood
was sawed off each side of the feet and hands and
split, in order to draw out the great iron spikes,
the young prince all the time standing by, weeping
and hurrying the men.   The older of the prisoners
was too far gone to be restored, and soon expired.
The younger, being about thirty years of age, revived, and in a few weeks was fully recovered.
This act of humanity procured for him the respect
and veneration of the whole empire.

Thur-ra-wa-di was proud, haughty, ambitious
and cruel.   It was well known in Ava that persons
whom he disliked had been betrayed into the compound and murdered by his orders.   Some of the
most noted robber chieftains in the empire were

known to be in constant communication with him, and had his protection; but the fact that he was the king's own brother, and shared largely in the king's confidence, was a sufficient reason why no officer of government should venture to impeach him. It was true this prince had some interesting traits of character, which, among a people like the Burmans, atoned for his faults. He was enterprising, enthusiastic and generous in his temperament. Those whom he esteemed he loaded with favors, and met them with fascinating smiles.

In February, 1837, a notorious robber chief, who had received for himself the title Kea-gee (the great tiger), was pursued by the government, and it was currently reported and believed that he had taken shelter with Prince Thur-ra-wa-di. A messenger was sent from the Lhoot dau (the king's high court), to the palace of Thur-ra-wa-di, to inquire if Kea-gee was there. This was an insult which the prince could not brook. He took fire instantly, and used insulting language to the court, at the head of which was the queen's brother, whom he hated as he did the queen, with a deadly hate.

The messenger fled back to the Lhoot dau, and

without loss of time an officer, with some eighty
or a hundred men, was sent to search for the robber chieftain. The prince, aware of what was
going on, armed between one and two hundred of
his men, and when the police arrived at his gate
and demanded admission, the prince ordered his
men to fire. Two or three were killed, several
wounded, and the rest fled precipitately to the
Lhoot dau. This was open rebellion. The whole
city was in an uproar. Thur-ra-wa-di, taking his
family and about three hundred men, forced one
of the gates of the city, and seizing whatever
boats they came to, crossed the river to Sagaing.
Taking the governor of that city and a few hundred men the prince went, by forced marches, to
Moke-so-bo, a strongly fortified city about fifty
miles west of Ava.

The reader will bear in mind that this is the
revolution inaugurated while Dr. Kincaid was in
the hands of the robbers in northern Burma.

From his new stronghold, Thur-ra-wa-di quickly
dispatched messengers through all the provinces
reporting that the queen's brother had usurped
the throne, imprisoned the king, murdered the
heir apparent, and was seeking to take his life; and

he called upon all to rally around his standard, and assist in putting down the queen's brother. The robber chieftains were dispatched to collect their hordes of outlaws together. In a few days he had about ten thousand armed men, and these were so placed as to cut off all communication between Ava and the provinces.

He had his spies constantly circulating reports in Ava, magnifying the number of his forces, and repeating his solemn oaths before pagodas that his only design was to put down the queen's brother and restore the king to his rightful power.

As the queen's brother was odious to the people generally, they were ready to believe any such reports.

This paralyzed the government; for though the king soon had some thirty thousand troops, and the walls of Ava bristling with cannon, it availed nothing. The people thought that in fighting Thur-ra-wa-di they were *really* fighting the king. So there was constant defection in the king's army. Early in May Ava was beleaguered. On every side was a large army, intent on plundering the capital. The Mekara prince was sent to intercede for the city. Thur-ra-wa-di insisted on giving it over to be sacked by his armies. Col. Burney, the English resident, was requested by the king to use his influence to save the city from the awful calamity threatened. Nothing could exceed the anxiety and gloom that reigned through the city. All business ceased. Old men sat in groups, conversing mournfully.

Mothers sat in their doors with their children nestled around them, listening to the thousand tales of outrage and cruelty committed without the walls the night before. The gaiety of the imperial city was gone. The walls were covered with troops, but no confidence was placed in them. All dreaded the approach of night, fearing an attack before morning.

Think of the lonely missionary's wife in these surroundings, without knowledge of the whereabouts or condition of the companion she was so wont to lean upon in hours of trial.

The king urged Colonel Burney, the English resident, to interpose his kind offices. Through his entreaties Thur-ra-wa-di spared the city. The keys of Ava were delivered to him, the king's troops were disbanded, and the whole empire was prostrated at his feet.

Soon the prisons of Ava were crowded with noblemen and officers who had been attached to the old government. In violation of oaths and promises the king was placed in confinement; the queen and her only daughter, about fourteen years of age, were trampled to death by elephants; the queen's brother, after suffering the most horrible tortures, was put to death. Public executions took place almost every day. Hordes of robbers over-run the land.

Thur-ra-wa-di tore in pieces the Yan-da-bo treaty, and told Colonel Burney that though he respected him as a man, as a British officer, yet as a resident at the court of Ava he did not know him.

About the same time he sent a special messenger to Dr. Kincaid to inform him that he must neither preach nor give sacred books to the people. "The next day," says Dr. Kincaid, "I waited on the new king to learn from his own lips his intentions on a subject so momentous as the closing of the empire against the diffusion of Christian knowledge. I was received as formerly, in the kindest manner, and he introduced the subject himself, in the presence of his whole court, by saying: 'The fates have made me king, and, therefore, I am

Tha-tha-na-da-ya-ka (defender of the faith), and must sustain the religion of the empire.'"

Much more was said in justification of the policy he purposed to pursue, not of sufficient importance to entitle it to space here.

The next day Dr. Kincaid called, taking with him a Burman Bible in four volumes. The king inquired very pleasantly, "What have you there?"

"The only book which the Eternal God has given to mankind," he replied.

The king directed an officer to take the book to his private apartments. He expressed a desire that Dr. Kincaid should remain in the capital, teach science, and translate for him the history of England. "I replied," says Dr. Kincaid, "that it was impossible for me to lay aside the office and work of a religious teacher."

The king's mind seemed made up that the Christian religion should not be taught, and his mind was as fully made up not to stay in Ava for any other purpose than teaching and preaching Christ.

"To act covertly, and try to accomplish something secretly, was foreign to my feelings, and in opposition to all my views of the spirit and genius of Christianity. We left Ava in sadness. We had

13

seen a little church grow up within the walls of
that ancient and proud city, large numbers had
become partially enlightened, and their minds
favorably impressed with the principles of Christianity.''

Mrs. Kincaid was almost daily surrounded with
females, who called to converse with her, and listen
to her instruction, and multitudes of old friends
gathered with the church and thronged the shore
the morning they left. The tears of sorrow told their
own sad story, while the tide bore them away from
the proud city. ''The thoughts and feelings of that
hour,'' says Dr. Kincaid, ''must remain unre-
corded.''

Ko-gway and his wife, two aged disciples, who
had endeared themselves to the missionaries by
their amiable manners and tender solicitude for their
happiness, spent a large part of the preceding day
at Dr. Kincaid's, rendering whatever assistance
they could. Several times they said, 'Teacher, we
shall pray that God will change the mind of the
king, or else take him away.'

Such were the feelings and prayers of many.
Thur-ra-wa-di· had put to death the heir-apparent,
the queen, her brother, and a large number of the

nobility and officers, all on whom there was the slightest taint of suspicion that they were favorable to the old government. He was not satisfied with removing the governors of provinces and cities; the greater number of them were brought to Ava in irons and then beheaded. One with whom Dr. Kincaid had been a guest, the governor of Mo-Nheen, a province near the borders of China, was brought to Ava in chains, and then fastened up to posts, and emboweled, near a great thoroughfare, just without the wall of the city, and when the missionaries left Ava, June 17th, the bones were still hanging there, rattling in the wind. He was a highly intelligent and venerable old man. The kindliness with which he had entertained Dr. Kincaid for a day and a night the preceding February, would do honor to a man of any nation.

His only crime was attachment to the old king. Neither faithfulness nor fitness for office was regarded — nearly all were swept away. Everything indicated that Thur-ra-wa-di would secure to his family an undisputed throne.

The Governor General of India took no notice of his spurning the English resident from his court, and his trampling under foot the treaty of Yandabo;

but, after some months, sent up another officer of high distinction, Colonel Benton, with a large amount in presents. The forbearance of the Governor General only increased his insolence. Colonel Benton could not obtain an audience, and the bazaar people were punished for selling provisions to Colonel Benton's servants, so that they were in danger of being starved. Colonel Benton, with his suite, was obliged to leave. After this, Thur-ra-wa-di proceeded to raise an army of 100,000 men, and all well armed, and proceeded to Rangoon, 500 miles from the capital.

With such a vast army hovering near the provinces ceded to the English, and led on by the king himself, no small anxiety was felt. To watch the movements of his army, cost the Indian government about half a million. After a few months' stay in Rangoon, the king, with his army, returned to Ava.

Passing by the Prince of Prome, a young man of fitness and successor to the throne, the king selected, and installed as his heir, a son of feeble intellect. The Prince of Prome was offended, and the Prime Minister, Moung-dau-gyee, manifested too openly his partiality for the prince, and was called to the palace. The king inquired if he was aware of the dissatisfaction of the Prince of Prome. The venerable old minister replied that he was. Instantly the king arose and stabbed his minister to the heart. Losing all self-control, and apparently becoming insane, he killed a large number of his principal officers. The Prince of Prome fled to the Shan provinces, east of Ava, but soon returned and was executed.

Among the ministers murdered was Mõung Gulla, a young man of rare talents, and the most distinguished military man in Burma. The remaining ministers and officers, fearing for their own safety, and regarding the king as insane, seized and confined him, and appointed a regency in which the Mekara prince had a conspicuous place, as also the old nobleman who had signed the Yandabo treaty.

Thus fell one of the proudest monarchs and one of the greatest tyrants that ever sat on the throne of Ava.

In eight short years he, with his family, passed from the summit of human ambitions to a felon's home.

The pacific and enlightened principles of government pursued before the revolution of 1837 were restored, and friendly relations again opened between Burma and India; the odious and crushing monopolies were removed, and commerce again flourished.

The Mekara prince was not a statesman, but was highly intelligent and enlighted, and humane and generous.   He had more knowledge of Christianity than any other prince in the empire, and was ft madness to believe that, in mercy to the millions of Burma, God raised him to power?   To the missionaries it seemed a most merciful interposition of divine providence, and opening up of the way to publish in the great and beautiful valley of the Irrawaddy the tidings of peace and salvation.

Then over all the mountain districts of Burma were thickly scattered the Karen villages, a people prepared in a remarkable degree for the reception of the gospel.   Would the church awake to more earnest prayer and vigorous efforts?   Would heralds of salvation respond to these providential calls and say ''*send me?*''

Dr. Kincaid was anxious to be off for his chosen field again as soon as he heard Mekara prince reigned instead of Thur-ra-wa-di.   Our next chapter will find him preaching the everlasting gospel to that people he longed to see saved.

CHAPTER XVIII.

ENROUTE AGAIN FOR BURMA.

"He is a chosen vessel unto me to bear my name before the Gentiles and Kings."—*Acts ix, 15.*

For several years it had been confidently asserted and published that Burma was forbidden the missionaries and further efforts to establish the new religion would not be tolerated.

But Dr. Kincaid so fully believed the time at hand to re-enter the field, that in 1849 he was led to ask from the Executive Committee an appointment as a missionary to Ava.

The Committee having complied with his request, he asked that a missionary physician might be sent to the same field at the same time.

Dr. Dawson, who applied for the apppointment, was peculiarly well fitted for the position, as he possessed an intimate acquaintance with the Burman people and understood their language. It was believed that his appointment would prove a protection to mission effort in Ava.

Notwithstanding these encouraging features and the fact that almost every pastor and many influential laymen of Philadelphia urged the appointment, the Committee did not feel justified to take a step incurring such expense without authority from the Board.   So at the annual meeting of the Missionary Union at Buffalo in 1850 the whole matter was laid before them and by them referred to a special committee, who through the Rev. Dr. Williams, made the following report.

"The subject," said they, "is one of grave import, and is not without its peculiar difficulties. The removal of aggressive operations on the part of our missions against the heathenism of Burma proper, has been for some years the theme of solicitude, discussion and prayer.   It seemed a reproach to American Baptists, that while their labors had been drawn off or excluded from their territories, some members of much older Romish missions remained in comparative security; although it was understood they so remained in virtual inertness, *mute* and *bound* as to any efforts at proselytism. Our own labors among the Karens, a noble though a subjugated race of the population of Burma, had been crowned with signal benediction; and the

recent journals of Roman Catholic missions show
that to this field, in which our triumphs have far
outstripped any Burman results of their labors, our
success has provoked them, and in consequence
Romish priests are now going thither to rival, to
thwart, and, if it may be, to supplant us."

The report here recognizes the work of Dr.
Kincaid in the east, and the years since spent at
home, "feeding and kindling missionary zeal in
his native country," but now, finding himself
ready to attempt a resumption of "his eastern
task," his heart yearned to preach Christ at Ava,
the imperial capital of Burma.   He desired that
most of his family accompany him, believing that
their presence might prove to the suspicious Burmans the honesty and unworldly character of his
mission.   They would be exposed, and at Ava far
from medical relief if sent out unprovided.

The applicant for appointment, Mr. Dawson, M.
D., had spent many years of his early life in Burma,
and spoke "several of its tongues"—was a skilled
physician of avowed piety and devotion.

Brethren of Philadelphia, who had known Dr.
Dawson more intimately during the years of his
residence there, urged even forcibly his appoint-

ment. But the committee at Boston found itself surrounded "with peculiar embarrassments." They must look with earnest solicitude to the results of adopting such a measure. Would it meet with the approval of the churches supplying the funds to carry forward the work?

Already they had spoken with some distinctness regarding the press, the school, and the tract, being used disproportionately. They wanted the simple preaching of the word, first middle and last, as the most prominent feature of missionary work.

Several of the missionaries in Burma dissented from Dr. Kincaid's opinion, that the time had come for the reopening of Ava to missionaries of the gospel.

The executive committee was willing for Dr. Kincaid to go forward, and if, on trial, his hopes were realized, he might then send back a statement, and the missionary physician should follow.

The cultivation of a "holy spirit of enterprise and a generous trusting faith in God are duties too often neglected by our churches. Again, faith rises almost to the point of rashness, dares the accomplishment of wonders, but ever should be submissive to the providences of God, and always active in the day of opportunity.''

After much deliberating and prayer, at last it was

"*Resolved*, That the board will sustain the executive committee in vigorous efforts to resume missionary operations in Burma proper, and will justify the committee in the appointment of a medical helper, to accompany the Rev. Dr. Kincaid in his attempts to re-enter that field, on such conditions as are suggested by the report of the committee of five on the part of this board.''

These instructions the executive committee com-complied with at once, and in July following Dr. Kincaid and family, accompanied by Dr. Dawson and family, embarked at Boston on the *Washington Allston*, arrived at Maulmain early in the year 1851. From this point he wrote, February 21:

There are difficulties to encounter in entering the work in Burma proper, but as yet they do not appear to be insurmountable. The reigning king manifested but little interest in government affairs, and his prime minister was reported to be a "peculiarly bigoted Buddhist.'' "On the other hand, persecution on account of religion had ceased, and the Christian Karens residing within the jurisdiction

of Burmese authority enjoyed a comfortable degree
of security and quietude.   It was also rumored that
there were, at that time, fifteen Burmese Christians
at the capital, one of whom was an officer of the
king, with a thousand men under his charge, and
another connected with the king's household ;
which seemed to imply, if the king was acquainted
with the facts, that he was not particularly hostile
to Christianity.

They tarried but eleven days in Maulmain, when
they took passage on a schooner of thirty-one tons,
manned by Mussulmen, reaching Rangoon March
5th, which Dr. Kincaid described as "little more
than one wide ruin" since the fire of the previous
December.   Not only had about three-fourths of
the city been swept by the devouring flames, but a
"great number of boats and several ships were
burned, hundreds of families barely escaping with
their lives."

Building was going on and men and material
were in demand

Koladan (or Foreigner's Street) escaped the
ravages of the fire. The buildings were owned
and occupied by Armenians, Mussulmans and
Hindoos. Dr. Kincaid went to the building

where he had lived nineteen years before, and
found it now occupied by a Hindoo who gave him
a cordial reception and a room to occupy while in
the city.

They showed themselves at the custom-house,
when they first landed and had their baggage
passed. A few hours later they were called for
and questioned regarding their business; where
they came from; the name of the ships; name of
the captain; at what places they had stopped
on the way; how many days they were in reaching Africa, the time they remained there; how
many days from Africa to Maulmain and how
many days they spent there, with many other
questions of a similar character; all was written
down with minuteness.

The next day they were sent for and questioned
regarding the object of their coming to Burma.
They were asked, "Are you Jesus Christ's men?"
all of which was written down, then read to them
and inquiry made as to the correctness of tran-
scribing.

Saturday of the same week they were sent
for again and questioned relative to Dr. Dawson's

knowledge of medicine, and how many kinds of diseases he could cure.

Dr. Dawson then showed them an illustrated volume on surgery. The officers examined the plates with care, and another record was made. The next morning the viceroy sent for Dr. Kincaid, who directed the secretary to inform his excellency that this was a sacred day, and that he could not attend to any worldly business. This seemed satisfactory until between nine and ten o'clock, when the secretary came and told Dr. Kincaid that he would be called for early next morning, and was to be questioned about his former residence in Ava. The secretary manifested no small degree of anxiety, thinking they were contriving some plan to get Dr. Kincaid into trouble. He was a fine young man, and appeared to be a true friend, but was very timid, more so, perhaps, because only a short time before an English merchant had been imprisoned and his feet put in the stocks because his father, as they alleged, had written a letter against the government that was published in one of the Calcutta papers. It cost him between five hundred and six hundred rupees to get out of prison. Several foreigners had been imprisoned during the past six months on the most frivolous pretenses, and money extorted from them. Early Monday morning Dr. Kincaid reported to the custom house to answer questions regarding his first years in Burma, how long he had lived in Rangoon, how long at Ava, and whatever seemed to them desirable to know, and all was carefully written down.

One of the officers apologized by saying it was done by order of the viceroy, whose authority was supreme. Dr. Kincaid replied that they had no objection to answering any questions the government was disposed to ask. They were treated very kindly by all the officials, who had known Dr. Kincaid before.

The viceroy was a new man, as also all the high officers of the empire.

The temper and policy of the government had changed amazingly since the revolution in 1837.

Ko Thah A, the venerable old pastor, called on them. The news of their arrival spread rapidly over the city and through the villages adjacent, and many called, among them two young men who had been educated in Mrs. Kincaid's school in Ava. Armenians, Mohammedans and Hindoos all visited the former teacher. A Jew, also, from Bagdad, spent two evenings listening to their account of the world's Messiah, and again the gospel was falling from consecrated lips upon ears not accustomed to hear these words that are "power" and "life."

CHAPTER XIX.

RESUMING WORK.

Dr. Kincaid visited Rangoon to learn whether it would be possible to get a house there for the use of his family, and, being successful, he returned at once to Maulmain. Soon after his return, reports were current in Maulmain that the governor of Rangoon had dealt severely with such persons as had shown the American teacher any favors during his short stay in Rangoon. These reports were accepted by many, from the start, as true, and soon were confirmed by letters from two Englishmen. The young Hindoo who had given him room in his house was thrown into prison, and compelled to pay a fine of two hundred rupees; while Moung-po-gyau, an interpreter, had his life threatened for daring to speak a word in his favor after he had gone.

This caused a diversity of opinion about the propriety of going to Rangoon in the face of such hostile measures.

To the mind of Dr. Kincaid, however, this opposition did not appear serious enough to delay for a day the execution of his plans, and accordingly he hastened his preparations to leave. Having engaged a schooner, they sailed on 'the 12th of April, and on the morning of the 16th lay at anchor before the great wharf.

The consternation consequent upon the arrival of the missionaries at Rangoon, and the difficulties that then immediately beset them, are related as follows in Dr. Kincaid's journal:

"It was thought extremely doubtful about our being allowed to land. On learning this, I was anxious to get all on shore before there would be time to issue an order prohibiting our landing. I hastened back to the vessel, and in a short time both families were in the house of Captain Potter. We returned as soon as possible, sent our beds, chairs, and a few boxes of clothing to the custom house, but it was near evening before they passed. Coolies were sent off with them to the house of Joe Alley, which we had rented before leaving Rangoon. When the old man saw the coolies loaded with baggage rushing into his compound, he and several servants raised a cry of alarm, and forbade a single article being put in the house. I came up just in time to prevent the coolies and baggage being thrust into the street. I remonstrated; told him he could not break his promise; that it was nearly dark, and that our ladies and children could not remain in the street. The poor old Mussulman stroked his long white beard, and trembled like an aspen leaf.

He was so agitated that he talked half Burmese and half Hindoostani, and kept saying over and over: "I am afraid—I am afraid of the governor. Moung Kinge has been imprisoned and fined two hundred rupees; a writer has been fined one hundred rupees, and Moung Poh Gyau has had his life threatened and has gone mad, and all on your account. I am afraid, sahib." His looks, his actions, his voice, all told how dreadfully frightened the old man was.

I told the coolies to put the things down and bring the remainder. The poor old man took hold of me in the most imploring manner, and begged me to have compassion on his grey beard. I told him I would stand between him and all harm. I was now here and the Governor would harm no one on my account. At length he gave a sort of consent to let us sleep one night in his house. Long after dark we had all assembled in the house and spread our mats on the floor.

Early on the morning of the 17th I went with Dr. Dawson on board the schooner, and began sending our boxes of books and medicines on shore, fearing, from all we heard, that an order might come prohibiting the landing of our baggage. We were delayed about boats and coolies, so that our baggage did ·not reach the custom-house until five o'clock, and but little of it was passed.

Joe Alley was more frightened than ever; he sent his son in the evening with two bottles of rose water, and told the governor that we had come into his house and he wished to get rid of us. The governor replied that he must send us off.

Early the next morning the governor came to the custom-house with a large retinue and we were summoned to appear before him.

There was a dense crowd, for his stern oppressive course against every one who had rendered us any little service, had awakened the greatest interest to know how he would proceed now that we had returned with our families and baggage. Besides Burmans there was a large number of for-

eigners, Mohammedans, Armenians and the few
English in the place. Without ceremony the governor began, in a loud, harsh tone of voice, to
question me about coming to Burma. "What
have you come here for? Who invited you?
Your object is to overturn the king's religion.
You have been driven out of Burma before. Who
gave you permission to come here?" and thus
he kept on for several minutes.

As soon as he gave me a chance to speak I
replied: "Your excellency must be aware that
when I lived in Ava I was on the most intimate
terms with nearly all the officers of the government, and was treated with the utmost kindness by.
the Mekara prince and Prince Thur-ra-wa-di.
When I left Ava the king urged me to remain, or
if I left, to return as soon as possible, and bring a
printing press and a physician. I promised to do
so, and have now returned as the king desired. So
far from being driven out of Burma, they urged
me not to go away."

His manner was at once changed. He began to
expatiate on the beauties of Buddhism, and said
that my object was to overthrow it. After a good
deal of this sort of thing he said: "You can remain

here, but you must keep in the house and do nothing till I get word from Ava." He then called a man who speaks Hindoostani as well as Burmese, and understands a little English, and said: "You must not enter a single house, or go abroad anywhere without having this man with you." Dr. Kincaid was told by several persons, not an hour after, that this man was one of the worst spies about the court, detested by all foreigners.

Things looked dark, much worse than had been anticipated. Having been requested to attend a funeral, Dr. Kincaid went, without paying the slightest regard to the spy who was to accompany him.

After the missionaries had withdrawn, the governor was violent in his expressions against Dr. Kincaid, and said before the whole crowd of people, foreigners and all, that he would not mind putting him in irons, but would be much pleased to have Dr. Dawson remain.

The threat to put Dr. Kincaid in irons spread like fire over the city, and on reaching Dr. Kincaid caused him to feel a perfect rush of indignation. Had the governor made the threat in his presence it would have been more manly, but to wait until he had gone from the gathering and then make such a threat plainly showed a spirit of cowardice and disposition to stab one in the back.

Dr. Kincaid's first thought was to tell the governor to his face the "contempt he felt for cowards and tyrants, but by the time the funeral, with all its solemnities, was over, he decided to pass the whole matter in silence."

"Poor old Joe Alley heard the news, and was thrown into a paroxysm of fear. His beard seemed to become whiter, and he looked as pale as death. All he could say was, 'Go! go! go!' so piteously that I could not withstand him. So, promising to get a place for our baggage, and to bring no more to his house, I started off at once. Of course I paid no attention to the governor's order to take his interpreter with me. It was, in fact, making me a prisoner, and I would recognize no such relation.

From an early hour a highly respected Mohammedan had been aiding us in every way he could. The governor noticed this in the afternoon and ordered him to be beaten. Instantly some three or four fellows pounced upon him, beat him in a savage manner, and kicked him out of the compound,—two hundred people looking on. I went to five or six places to procure store room, as our baggage was being rapidly overhauled and tumbled unceremoniously out of the custom-house.

On Saturday it was all passed and safely stowed in Captain Potter's godown. During the day a number of respectable persons, Burmans and foreigners, urged us to go to the governor and 'speak sweet words to him,' but I resolved to seek no interview. On Monday, however, at the urgent request of many, we concluded to go, and started off, but learned on the way that the governor was in a terrible passion, and had that morning beaten a Mussulman terribly. At five o'clock, P. M., we set off again, but being informed that about an hour before the same man was beaten so dreadfully that he was carried off to die, we postponed our visit. The next morning we started off again and again turned back, having learned that the governor, that very morning, had had a serious quarrel with his principal wife. A report was current in the city on Monday evening and through the following day, that the governor had publicly threatened my life. I did not then, and do not yet, believe there was sufficient ground for such a

report.   But, true or not true, I was fully satisfied
that he was too cowardly to commit such an outrage, and would have cared little about it had
it not reached my family.''

We now relinquished altogether the idea of
going to him, but about seven in the evening word
came from the governor requesting us to call. We
resolved at once to go, though it was very dark and
two miles off. We found him in an inner apartment, with two or three officers and a few servants,
He treated us courteously, and showed us several
swords made by a Burman. He wished us to praise
them, and really the workmanship was praisewor-
thy. He made many inquiries about my former
acquaintances in Ava. After a little while we got
into an animated conversation about men and
things in the Golden City. I told him it was my
intention to go up to Ava after the rains, to which
he made no reply. We remained about an hour.
When we were about leaving he said: ''I shall
write to the king and make strong representations
in your favor; but there is one thing you must
promise, that is, to give no tracts to the people.''
I did not ask him for permission to remain; I did

not ask him to write to the king; still, I thanked him for his offer to write.

We had that very day rented the house formerly occupied by Colonel Burney, now owned by Moung Sa, an aged Woon-gee in Ava. Without our knowledge the agent came in to obtain the governor's sanction, which was given promptly. Then turning to us he said: "That is a very suitable house for you." All passed off very well. After spending a week of anxiety, the storm seemed to have spent itself.

*   *   *   *   *   *

On the 3rd of May a Sera-dau-gyee came, by order of the governor, to inform us that a royal message had that day arrived; that the king had heard with pleasure of the American teachers who formerly lived in Ava; he expressed a wish that they would be disposed to remain in Burma, and that they might enjoy every possible favor. The royal secretary was attended by a large retinue, and he seemed much gratified that he was the bearer of such news.

The large hall in our house having been put in order, I preached in English and in Burmese the first Lord's day in May, and had about thirty hearers; among them were three Karens, residing about two days' journey from Rangoon. One of them had been two years in Brother Binney's school, and was an intelligent young man. He was the pastor of a church in the village where he lived. He inquired earnestly and affectionately after Brother Binney and Brother Vinton. In the evening we had a prayer meeting—four prayers in Burmese, one in Karen, and one in English; also, singing in three languages.   *   *   *   *

Poor Moung Kinge died three days ago, and on the following day was followed to the grave by a large number of people. He was much respected by the entire community. This was the second man murdered by the governor after our arrival at Rangoon. One was whipped to death and Moung Kinge was frightened to death. From the day he was imprisoned, his life menaced, and the threat ferociously made that his wife and children should be made slaves and sent in chains to Ava, Moung Kinge sank gradually to the grave. He had no fortitude, and the shock was too great for him. The bitter tears of his widow and children awakened in me the emotions of unutterable detestation toward the brutal tyrant who caused so much suf-

fering, Mounge Kinge's crime was giving Dr.
Dawson and myself the use of a room seven or
eight days; for this he was frightened to death.

Moung Poh Gyan barely survived the savage
treatment he received.   Gladly would I have been
in the place of these young men, and suffered all
the indignities and cruel threats of the governor.

Ko A, the venerable old pastor, called occasion-
ally, in good health but infirm with age.   The
church was scattered in different villages, except a
few superannuated members.   Ko A was too feeble
to labor.   The condition of the Karens was little
known in this and the neighboring province of
Bassein, up to this time.   The greater number of
the Karen churches were from forty to one hundred miles distant.

This brief outline of events since we landed
in the city one month ago, must suffice now.   You
will perceive that a great change has taken place
toward us on the part of the government, much to
the astonishment of all, Burmans and foreigners.
We may meet with opposition, we may expect it,
but still, with the divine blessing, nothing is too
great to be overcome.   I preach just as openly as I
ever did in any land.   So far we feel encouraged

and hope that the Lord has heard our prayers, and the prayers of his people in behalf of these millions. Pray for us that we may be wise in winning souls to Christ.''

CHAPTER XX.

IN FAVOR WITH THE PEOPLE.

"When a man's ways please the Lord, He maketh
even his enemies to be at peace with him."—*Prov. xvi. 7.*

In addition to the order from Ava, which reached
Rangoon on the third of May, and to which reference was made in the preceding chapter, the
governor subsequently received another communication from the king, and Dr. Kincaid was immediately summoned by the viceroy to listen to the
reading of the royal letter.

When assembled in full court, and the missionary
presented himself, as directed, a secretary, by the
governor's directions, read aloud:

"The American teachers shall be allowed, if
they wish, at any time they may choose, to come
up to the *golden feet;* or, if they prefer remaining
in Rangoon, are not to be molested."

After the reading of this royal order the missionaries at once commanded universal respect, and one
could hardly fancy the altered tone of the officers

and people towards the teachers. Before the orders came and were read, the officers and people were haughty and proud and insolent. Even the coolies in the streets would take pains to jostle the missionaries, while the underlings in office were insolent in the extreme. But after the reading of the order this was no longer so.

This order from Ava was unsolicited and unexpected, so that they could regard it in no other way than an indication of Providence for them to go forward in their work.

The object of Dr. Kincaid in returning to Burma was well understood. The governor himself said it was to overcome the king's religion. Of our mission, the character of our books and the peculiarities of our religion much was said that was true.

They asked many questions, among them, Are you "Jesus Christ's men?" Dr. Kincaid said yes, and I will give you the reason, and he proceeded to set forth, in a talk of twenty-five minutes, an outline of the Christian religion, without interference on the part of any one.

On the 29th of July they were notified that the governor expected to see them.

He had kindly sent up a petition to the king, at great expense had brought the royal order from Ava, and expected a neat sum to drop into his coffers.   And Dr. Kincaid said to the messenger: "You may tell the governor that it is an outrage to speak of expense."

"I dare not speak such words, for he is the governor, and you had better see him."

"Very well, but not to-day."

It was expected that a demand would be made on the missionaries for money, amounting to about one hundred dollars, and Dr. Kincaid was asked, in case of such a demand, what he should do. "Refuse to pay any such demand."

It was urged, as governor, he had power to compel.   To which Dr. Kincaid replied:

"He has power to send us out of the country, but has not power enough to compel us to submit tamely to extortion and oppression."

They remained quiet two or three days, feeling no anxiety to rush matters.   But were urged by some friendly natives that it would be best to see the governor, taking a present worth fifteen or twenty dollars, and tell the governor that they

were afraid and poor, and throw themselves on his
clemency.

Neither is true, was Dr. Kincaid's reply.   We
are not afraid, nor are we so poor as to beg.   Had
the governor a just claim we would pay it, but will
not tamely submit to tyranny, which would be only
to invite outrage and oppression.

On July 31st, Dr. Kincaid appeared before the
governor with a present worth about eight rupees,
four dollars.   They were very kindly received, and
among other inquiries made was when the missionaries intended going to Ava.   When informed they
purposed going at the close of the rainy season,
"You are right," said the governor.   "It is both
difficult and dangerous to go up during the rains.
When you are ready to go I shall furnish you with
the expense of the journey."

No one who saw him would have supposed him
to be the governor, with whom they had to deal
only about three months before.

While disposed to be somewhat conciliatory in
his personal relations, he seemed anxious, also, to
convey an impression that his views were to a
degree changed respecting Christianity; and speak-

ing to Dr. Kincaid one day on the subject, in the presence of the court, he said:

"One thing about your religion I do not like. It aims to destroy every other, and that is uncharitable. Your religion is good, but you allow not ours to be good." To this Dr. Kincaid replied as follows: "Christianity designs to bring all mankind to love God supremely, and to love others as themselves. This makes men wise, and good, and happy."

"You are getting all the people over to your side," said the governor, "for you make them think well of yourselves and of your doctrine."

The intolerant spirit of Christianity was to many a reason for rejecting it; whereas they should have seen in its purpose to supplant every other religion —to have the whole heart or none—its purpose to perpetuate purity of heart and life in its adherents in all lands, and not compromise and destroy its purity by adopting from this religion enough to please and win its old adherents; enough of that to make it popular with the masses, and leave them in a state of delusion. The Eternal God must be the real object of all true worship—the Holy Spirit leading us through the Son from death and sin into life and fellowship with God, and adding us thus to the number of the ransomed, robed in the righteousness of Calvary.

"An official high in rank said: 'These teachers have all sorts of books, and maps of all the countries of the world, and globes that represent the earth as round as an orange, and that it turns round every day, and that the sun stands still. Does not this go to destroy Gaudama's religion?"

"True," said the governor; "this makes our religion false."

Dr. Kincaid replied: "Whether the sun goes round the earth or the earth around the sun, is a question that belongs to science and not to religion."

God favored and strengthened the faith of Dr. Kincaid, and we find him enlisted for the evangelization of Rangoon, and for the spread of the gospel through the whole length and breadth of the empire.

The scattered members of the Burman church now began to gather round him; representatives of churches from distant towns came in to express their congratulations. Others called to solicit books, and on every hand he was permitted to see the most cheering tokens of the divine favor.

"The native brethren sent to visit the Karen churches east of Rangoon, and north and northwest, brought back most cheering reports, stating that in every Christian household they found family worship maintained morning and evening, and on each first day of the week they, met four times for public service.

The news of Dr. Kincaid's arrival at Rangoon had preceded these messengers, and when these devoted native Christians heard how roughly the authorities treated Dr. Kincaid, they prayed.incessantly that he might not be driven from the country.

In one village they spent a Lord's day with a church numbering more than four hundred members and when they learned from the letters borne by these messengers that they were constantly remembered in the prayers of the teachers, they were moved to tears and many wept aloud for joy. From the pastor of this church they bore to Dr. Kincaid the following simple and touching letter.

"May the grace and fellowship of the Father, Son and Holy spirit be with you, with my love and the love of all the sons and daughters of this church. I am one of the least of all the disciples and know but little of the divine word. Divine grace has made me a teacher of the gospel, and by the sacred imposition of hands I am made a pastor. Daily I study the Bible and pray for a larger measure of the Holy Spirit, so as to teach and guide this flock of little ones.

I have but little knowledge and can teach only what I know. I, the pastor, and all the church rejoiced greatly when we heard that you had come into this Burman kingdom, and cease not to pray for you. Our Father who is in heaven will hear our prayers.

We all desire to see you, and to hear more fully the deep things of God, that we may grow and be established in every virtue.''

The ardent love of the Karens for the gospel was never more strikingly illustrated than in the efforts and sacrifices many made, about this time, to possess portions of the word of God. Some came from a great distance, through districts infested with robbers and amidst almost incessant storms.

Among these, Dr. Kincaid makes special mention of two Christian boys from the province of Pautanan, one hundred and thirty miles from Rangoon. They had been sent by the church, with a letter, requesting ten New Testaments, a copy of Pilgrim's Progress, seven tracts and two hymn books.

The books were carefully rolled up and put in the bottom of a basket, and then the basket filled with rice and dried fish.   This done, they gave the parting hand, and, in tremulous voice said, "Pray for us that we may be delivered from the calamity of falling into the hands of officers with these books."

Toward the close of the year inquirers multiplied and numbers of hopeful converts presented themselves for baptism.

One, in relating the exercises of his mind, said that, about three months previous, his heart was much perplexed through a dream.   He imagined himself going toward Shway Dagong, and when not far off it crumbled down into a mass of ruins. He woke up in great distress, feeling that all his life long he had been rendering the homage due only to God, to that senseless mass of ruins.   He betook himself to prayer and the reading of the New Testament.

The light of truth shined in upon his soul, and he found peace in believing.

Says Dr. Kincaid, our baptism took place between three and four o'clock in the afternoon, in the royal tank, a beautiful, clear sheet of water, nearly four miles in circumference. It contained several finely wooded islands, and was surrounded on three sides by groves having a park-like appearance.

Under the deep, dark foliage of a clump of aged trees, on the green bank, sloping down to the water's edge, with the glittering spires of a hundred pagodas before them, they kneeled in prayer to Him who said, 'Lo I am with you.' The depth of feeling and joy of heart felt on that occasion, as four Burmans and five Karens went down into the baptismal grave, rendering homage to Him who is the 'resurrection and the life,' no tongue can tell nor artist paint.

Earnest inquirers received the word of God into their hearts, and numbers no longer attempted any defense of the old religion, but were free to say 'Gaudama cannot stand.'

After having Gaudama's religion for a thousand years, we are a poor ignorant people.

Fields were whitening for the harvest on every

hand, with no serious opposition to missionary efforts.   People of all ranks and conditions were now coming as earnest seekers after truth and salvation.   An officer of high rank, with his wife and twenty-five or thirty attendants, called one evening on Dr. Kincaid and his family, and gave them very urgent invitations to return the call.

CHAPTER XXI.

LABORS INTERRUPTED BY WAR.

While diligently preaching God's message of love,
The war cloud covered the heavens above;
The roar and the rattle of saber and gun
Told Dr. Kincaid, there preaching was done
'Till the war cloud burst, or moved on its way,
And no one could tell how long it might stay.
Of the harvest, he, there, had already sown,
What portion the Lord would get for His own;
So he turned for a time away from the cloud,
The roar of the battle so fearful and loud,
And cheerfully sowed in Maulmain the seed
That was then, as now, the heathen world's need.
The battle still raged, the field was o'erspread
With bodies of wounded, of dying and dead,
And all day long 'mid the dying he went,
As an angel of love to sufferers sent,
Binding the wound, and pointing the soul
To Jesus, who makes men every whit whole;
Catching the sad, low-whispered farewell
As the soul took its flight for heaven or hell.

During a residence of more than six months in
Rangoon, Dr. Kincaid had been cheered by scenes
and incidents of extraordinary interest; but in the
midst of these encouragements, and when he had
nearly completed preparations for proceeding to the

capital in pursuance of his original purpose, and
under favor of the royal invitation, a new aspect
was put on the posture of things by the arrival of
a war steamer at Rangoon, demanding on behalf of
the East India government, redress of grievances.
For a long time British subjects had suffered from
the Burmese government the greatest injustice.
Without cause they had often been fined and
imprisoned, and, such was the terror under which
they were living, that they were compelled to
endure these wrongs in silence, knowing that the
slightest whisper of dissatisfaction would only be
visited by ten-fold greater outrages, and even with
cruel tortures and death.   At length tidings of the
doings of the government towards British subjects
reached the ears of Commodore Lambert, and,
after taking the necessary steps to satisfy himself
of the truth of these reports, he came to demand
redress of the Burmese authorities.

The immediate cause of Commodore Lambert's
appearance in Rangoon with his ships of war, was
a statement verified as correct and signed by Dr.
Kincaid.

While the English merchants residing at Rangoon were familiar with the deeds of injustice and

violence inflicted on their own countrymen by the Burmans, they were there to make money and not to right the wrongs inflicted on their countrymen.

The English resident was powerless without a statement of grievances to give relief. This statement the merchants with one consent declined to make.

When the matter became intolerable, and one ship owner had been compelled to pay 6,000 rupees ($3,000) without one provoking cause, Dr. Kincaid was commenting on the situation of affairs and asked the English resident why he did not seek relief for his countrymen. "Not a merchant," said Col. Burney, "will make a statement," lest it injure his business. "Well," said Dr. Kincaid, "write up the facts and I will sign a statement." By this he became, using his own words, "the top, bottom and sides of a war between Burma and England." One hour longer on shore would have made him a prisoner of war. His library and household effects were scattered and destroyed; and while there was no law in England allowing him to be paid for his effects, Parliament made an exception in Dr. Kincaid's case and in some measure compensated him for his losses, which aided in making comfortable his declining years.

On the evening of the 24th of November, 1851, a frigate and four armed steamers came before the city and immediately everything was thrown into the utmost state of alarm. The governor threatened to set the city on fire, and in every house the foreigners were at work securing their papers and property. Great gongs were beating in every direction. A report was current that all who wore hats (Europeans) would be seized and carried off as hostages. Near midnight Dr. Kincaid was sent for to go to the governor's, nearly two miles distant. Without hesitation he set off, but was met by messengers countermanding the order. On the following morning the governor, with a large guard, appeared on the wharf, and there issued an order that any person, foreigner or native, who should come down to any of the wharves, or appear on the bank of the river, should be instantly beheaded. This order was published through the city by beat of gong and public crier. On hearing this Dr. Kincaid went immediately to the main wharf, where there were several distinguished officers and a guard, and remonstrated with them in strong terms on the insane course they were pursuing—working themselves and the people into a panic, when there was all possible evidence that the ships were come on a peaceful mission—to prevent, not to make war. They felt it, but were disposed to be blind to the innumerable acts of injustice and cruelty inflicted on all classes of people.

Commodore Lambert having sent a deputation of four officers, with a communication to the viceroy, he immediately called for Dr. Kincaid, and in the presence of some fifty of his great chiefs, desired to know from him whether the translation of the commodore's letter was correct. After carefully reading both he was assured that it had been faithfully rendered. "What does it mean?" said the governor. "I am accused of being a bad man, committing outrages on Her Britannic Majesty's subjects, and yet the letter does not specify in what way I have done this. Tell me what I should do."

"I am not competent," said Dr. Kincaid, "to advise in these matters."

"Do not tell me so," he said, "you have more books and maps than all the other people in the city, and you know what the English want and what I can do."

To get rid of his importunities Dr. Kincaid said: "You can write to the commodore and ask for an explanation."

This struck him favorably. Then he inquired whether the English came for peace or war. "For peace undoubtedly," Dr. Kincaid replied. "If they had come for war, instead of three or four ships they would have had twenty-five or thirty."

"After a few days," says Dr. Kincaid, in his journal, "the governor recovered in some measure from the panic into which he was thrown, and commenced hostile preparations, buying up all the muskets in the city, collecting guns from all the neighboring cities, and fortifying the heights of Shway Dagong, and building stockades at Kee-men-ding, four miles above the city. He collected from the surrounding villages about ten thousand men, and invited to his aid a celebrated robber chief with all his followers, thus getting together all the desperate characters of the lower provinces. As yet we felt safe in the city, as the majority of the inhabitants were foreigners, but on the 4th and 5th of December orders were issued, it was reported, to attack the foreigners, plunder them, cut their throats, and burn the city. Bodies of armed men and of desperate characters were constantly parading the streets. Foreigners were all armed, and keeping ceaseless watch on their houses.

Commodore Lambert very kindly gave me an invitation to place the ladies and children on board of one of his vessels, and the stern cabins of the steamer *Tenasserim* were prepared for them; but Captain Baker, of the *Duchess of Argyle*, a large merchant ship, invited us to take refuge in his vessel, which seemed preferable, as the ships of war were threatened with an attack by fire-rafts. On the evening of the 5th we took Mrs. Kincaid and Mrs. Dawson, with the little children, to a private wharf, where a boat was ready to take them on board the *Duchess*. The next day the young ladies went on board, Dr. Dawson and myself remaining on shore most of the time. We packed up our books and the most valuable part of our baggage, and placed them in fire-proof godowns belonging to Mr. Birrell. The ladies and children were now safe, and there was little danger to our property from fire, but it was necessary to keep a constant watch, especially by night, as the governor

threatened to turn loose these robbers, now about
500 strong. He had openly and repeatedly declared
his intention of taking the lives of eight persons,
whom he named, among whom I was included.
We regarded his threats as the ravings of a mad-
man ; still kept away from the new city, for I knew
if he should muster courage to commence hostilities, he would be anxious to have me for a translator
and interpreter.

    *   *   *   *   *   *

A little after dark on the 10th of December, as
I was passing along one of the principal streets, I
was suddenly seized by some eight or nine Burmans,
who partly carried, partly dragged me into a dark,
narrow lane. There I was surrounded by forty or
fifty armed men. A long and not very pleasant
altercation followed, they threatening me, and I,
in turn, threatening them; they insisting on taking
me to the governor, and I insisting on going to the
custom house. At length I got to the custom
house. I hardly know how. A bundle of clothes
from the washerman, which a Burman carried after
me, was the excuse for this outrage. The custom
house officers interfered, and, after a long dispute,
these guards went to the governor for an order to

take me out. It was nearly two miles to the governor's, and while they were gone the custom house officers hurried me off on board ship.

This, it seems, annoyed his excellency, for the next afternoon he sent an officer to the commodore complaining that I had taken my family aboard ship without his permission, and so had broken the laws of Burma. Commodore Lambert replied that that law might hold in reference to Burman subjects, but not in reference to British subjects or persons claiming British protection. He drew up a letter and sent it to the governor by one of his officers and Mr. Edwards, his translator, in which he stated, that the amity existing between the government of the United States and Her Britannic Majesty rendered it imperative on his part to demand of his excellency the punishment of those men who had seized and maltreated me the evening before, in the streets of Rangoon. The governor expressed much regret at what had taken place, and said the men should be punished, If I would point them out. Of course this was impossible, for the men were withdrawn from the old city.

The following is a copy of the letter addressed
16

by Commodore Lambert to the governor of Rangoon:

JASON M. SOUTHEY, Secretary:

On board Her Britannic Majesty's ship of war *Fox*, at anchor off the town of Rangoon, 10th of December, 1851.

To the Governor of Rangoon:

It having been represented to me by the Reverend Mr. Kincaid, a native of the United States of America, who is now living on board the British ship *Duchess of Argyle*, that while on the pier at Rangoon, last night, as he was about to embark to join his family, he was seized by some persons said to be in the employ of the Burmese government, and grossly insulted while being conveyed to the custom house, where he was detained for two hours. In the absence of any representative of his country, a nation in cordial alliance with Her Britannic Majesty, I call on you, as governor of Rangoon, to cause inquiry to be made, and to punish the offenders who have dared to insult this gentleman, and also to take measures to prevent a recurrence of such disgraceful conduct.

I have the honor to subscribe myself,

(Signed)   GEORGE ROBERT LAMBERT,

Commodore, in charge of Her Britannic Majesty's Naval Forces, employed on these coasts.

On the 12th I went on shore again. I had learned that three Portuguese, the tools of a Jesuit, had made the governor believe that I was at the bottom of the English expedition. This was the secret of his hostility to me.

Within a few days the governor of Dalla received orders to place his troops at the disposal of the viceroy of Rangoon. Accordingly, fifteen hundred men crossed the river early on the morning of the 19th, uttering the most savage yells. On the 18th one thousand men arrived from Prome. After all, the only men the governor could depend on were the robbers. The peasantry, that made up four-fifths of his army, would throw away their muskets and run at the firing of the first gun. The officers threatened to place Karen Christians in the fore front of the battle if the English came on shore. Three hundred of the disciples were on duty at the great pagoda. The churches were sending messengers to us almost daily to inquire how things were, and to let us know their situation. Few of them slept in their houses for fear of robbers. Our hearts bled for them. We could only say to them, "Look to Him who took care of Elijah in the desert." The Burman peasantry, heathen as well as Christian, were also sending messages to us, expressing the hope that the English would put an end to the brutal tyranny under which they had suffered so long. Among our more than ten thousand disciples, besides hundreds who were "almost Christians," there was earnest prayer to Him who ruleth over all.

Through a merciful providence we had not left for Ava. We had procured one boat, and were just settling the price of another, when the war ships arrived. The Lord "ordereth all things well."

As every effort for amicable adjustment failed, war was inevitable. The mission families were in peril, and had only one hour to take refuge on ship board.

One hour more and we would have been prisoners. Many foreigners failed to escape and were loaded with chains and crowded into loathsome prisons. Some died under their sufferings and others were repeatedly ordered out for execution and then remanded to prison."

As it was impossible to calculate how long these hostilities would continue, the missionaries deemed it prudent to seek a refuge in Maulmain.

After remaining there about three months, however, Dr. Kincaid, leaving his family behind him, determined to return to Rangoon. The very day of his arrival the war was virtually terminated by the destruction of the great fortress, which had been defended by 30,000 Burmans, with over two hundred mounted guns. "From seven o'clock in the morning till evening of that day," says Dr. Kincaid, "I spent in the field-hospital among the wounded and dying. At night I walked back two miles to the ship, among the dead and dying Burmans strewed on the battlefield. That was a terrible day, and I thought continually of our suffering disciples. After all, their sufferings had hardly begun. The great Burman army was shattered into fragments, and now, in groups of from one to three hundred, they were ravaging the country, burning villages, slaughtering the cattle and robbing the people. I took up my abode in an old building, having a great number of idols in it. Having cleared out the idols and cobwebs, one large room was converted into a chapel. A Karen deputation found me the third day after the battle, and then there was coming and going in one continued stream. The Burman disciples, also, came in from their various hiding places, and with them many other Burmans took refuge under my building."

In the following June, Dr. Kincaid was again joined by his family from Maulmain, and, having set things in order, every department of missionary work moved on as they never had seen it before. The people's hearts were softened like wax. The arm of the Lord was laid bare, and they had Pentacostal seasons and baptisms every Sunday. From several villages where we sent preachers and school teachers, came cheering accounts. Two entire villages turned their buildings into chapels and school houses, and sent to us a request to be taught the ways of God more perfectly.

Within a few days they had buried two Christian women, one of them the oldest member of the church, about ninety-three years of age. Till the very last she retained her mental powers remarkably. She possessed much faith, and spoke often of her desire to depart and be with Christ. At the last communion season she was borne to the chapel, and at the close expressed her joy at being once more permitted to unite in this holy service.

We learned from Mr. Marshman, of Serampore

editor of the *Friend of India*, that about this time
the principles of Christianity had taken deep root
in the hearts of some 12,000, and through these a
large amount of moral influence was brought to
bear on thousands more. The churches were scat-
ered all the way from the seaboard to Prome. They
now had at school in Rangoon two hundred and
fifty young persons, preparing to go back to their
villages, some to teach and preach among their
countrymen. About forty native preachers were
supported by congregations over the country. The
intelligence of recent events in Burma had aroused
to new energy the friends of missions in America,
and Dr. Kincaid had no doubt but they would be
sustained by needful aid. It was his hope to see
churches raised up along the whole line of this
river to the Hukang valley. Then they could
stand on the borders of Western China, and on the
upper waters of the great Cambodia, and could
reach, by books and preaching, untold millions in
the center of Eastern Asia. He said once, that he
almost wished he had been born thirty years later
in the Christian era, that he might have seen
Christianity pouring its light over these vast
regions; yet he could but trust the execution of

his cherished plans to those who should come after
him to gather the bounteous harvests ripening to
the gleaner's hand.

CHAPTER XXII.

NEGLECTED PROME—A PROMISING FIELD.

"Declare ye among the nations, and publish, and set up a standard; publish and conceal not."—*Jeremiah l,2.*

How dark the days stretched into years,
  Where Jesus was not known;
How warm with love the prayers and tears
  Poured on the word there sown.
Before that waste and barren field
  Sighed for the reaper's hand,
To garner for God the gracious yield
  Ripening in all the land;
And waiting the gleaner's work of love
  To place the sheaves in store,
For transit up to the world above,
  Secure forever and ever more.

Prome, a city of fifty thousand inhabitants, midway between Rangoon and Ava, in 1853 gave promise of a most fruitful center from which to disseminate the gospel. Dr. Judson had preached there in 1830 for a short time, with bright prospects of success, but, after a few months stay, was ordered away, after which time but little effort had been made to establish gospel missions in Prome.

Dr. Kincaid made this long-neglected city his

home and laid plans in strong faith for its evangelization.   He was kindly assisted by the Quarter-
master General of the army in obtaining two
monasteries, with a zayat convenient for public
service, where on January 22nd, 1853, was held
the first public religious service.

A convert whom Dr. Kincaid had baptized ten
years before in Arracan, was already holding
nightly meetings in his own home; and, being
assistant commissioner at Prome, enjoyed a position that gave him influence and the opportunity
of doing much good for his countrymen.

Dr. Kincaid soon began holding services in a
chapel near the center of the city, where from one
hundred to one hundred and fifty attentive hearers
assembled, besides comers and goers to near an
equal number.   At the close of morning service,
many would stay for an after meeting, in which
the native disciples would gather into groups of
five or ten persons, and in a conversational way lay
before their hearers the claims of the gospel, and
the advantages of a Christian life.   These meetings were often of the deepest interest, sometimes
lasting for hours, and the Bible was frequently
appealed to in settling questions when different

views were held. This revealed the fact, first, that the people were inquiring, and secondly, that the Bible was coming to be accepted as authoritative.

On February 27th three converts were baptized as the first fruits of the gospel. By July following the number had increased to thirty-eight, with inquirers multiplying on every hand. Frequent excursions were made into the adjacent villages, sometimes by the natives only, at other times by the missionaries, who were encouraged to find such readiness on the part of the people to accept the gospel. Forty miles below Prome, at Keaugen, a city of sixty thousand people, multitudes gave ear to the gospel. Buddhism was crumbling, and gospel churches springing up. Two Karen and two Burman churches had now been planted, with promise of a fifth. Eighty converts had been admitted to baptism, two of whom came from the capital to learn more perfectly the way of life. The church at Prome had grown in strength and influence, and now numbered seventy members.

Innumerable villages covered the country, which caught the infection, and natives were giving them-

selves to study preparatory to preaching the gospel
and aiding the missionaries to gather the whitening
harvest from the constantly ripening field.

The prayer and hope of the missionaries now
were that the Lord would raise up laborers to reap
the harvest of souls ripening to the gleaner's hand.

Dr. Kincaid was much encouraged by the large
proportion of gifted converts coming to Jesus.
Public meetings by the natives were now frequent,
and often crowded until many were turned away
for lack of room. The Macedonian cry came ring-
ing from every quarter until Dr. Kincaid said: ''I
feel oppressed beyond utterance when I look over
this wide field and see what is to be done. It is
important that we employ all the sanctified talent
within our reach for evangelizing these cities and
villages.'' For years he had longed and prayed
for the very things that now overwhelmed him.
What he most desired to see became a burden too
great for human strength, and his longing now was
for reapers and gleaners. For months his journals
show no abatement of interest, but a continuance
of the work of grace, so that many converts were
baptized. In this year the first Chun convert was
baptized. The Chuns were a branch of the great

Karen family, and occupied the Yuma Mountains for hundreds of miles.

Of the Karen field Dr. Kincaid said it was large to the south-east and to the north-east and the spirit of inquiry increasing. They had baptized more than forty Karen converts and had eight in training for teachers and two for assistants. But this must prove an inadequate number for the rapidly widening field everywhere demanding the reaper's toil and the husbandman's care.

Karen chiefs were making frequent personal calls for teachers to instruct the people in the truths that make wise unto salvation. They were not blind to the improved condition of those whose God was the Lord. This sanction of the chiefs made the masses free and anxious to prosecute their inquiries, so that Dr. Kincaid said that in every direction the influence of the gospel was spreading and converts were multiplied in all the adjacent towns and villages.

While all these encouraging features gave such promise of success among the Karens, there was a very encouraging feature in the work at Prome because of the number of Burman converts who were not only acknowledging Christ, but were

faithfully living for his cause and truth.   They, as
a rule, were much slower to accept salvation than
the Karens but of the one hundred and sixty-one
converts baptized by the end of the year, more
than one hundred were Burmans.

Another encouraging feature of the work at
Prome was the large proportion of gifted men and
women converted.   Every evening one and often
two public meetings were held in the city, generally conducted by Ko Dway and Moung Pan-te.
Often these gatherings were so crowded that many
were turned away for want of room.   Other
natives were constantly going from village to
village and city to city preaching the gospel of
Jesus.

A large part of Dr. Kincaid's work now was
superintending and guiding the native toilers in
their labors, so blessed of heaven on every hand.
In a letter, bearing date October 3, 1889, from one
whose father was also a missionary on the same
field, it is said, "His time was spent in traveling
from town to town and from village to village,
preaching to Burmans, Karens, Shyens, Shans,
wherever he could find an audience, whether of
one or one hundred, he gave them the gospel."

"He was a splendid horseman, and invariably rode at a 'break-neck' pace. When about to start off in the rain, he would refuse the offer of an umbrella, saying, 'I'll ride between the drops,' and it looked as though he did."

He was a very active man, whose zeal for souls was very ardent to the last, and only permitted his retirement from active service when frail nature had given way under the weight of years of toil. His soul was delighted to hear of prosperity in the cause of Christ, in any land, with any people.

He never had trouble with the Board of the Missionary Union, but manfully stood up and defended his brethren on a foreign field who had trouble. He ever did what he believed to be right without fear or favor.

> How reviving when we hear
> Words of comfort, words of cheer,
> How the gospel wins its way,
> Turning darkness into day.
> From end to end of that great land,
> Where high Pagodas thickly stand,
> Jesus now is sought and owned.
> While dumb idols are dethroned,
> See Christ, our king, in Burma stay,
> O'er the empire gaining sway.
> As king of kings where He is known,
> The people love His name to own.

CHAPTER XXIII.

IN FAVOR WITH THE KING.

"Seest thou a man diligent in his business, he shall stand before kings."—*Prov. xxii, 29.*

He did his work with all his might,
Nor ever faltered in the right;
This only question would he ask,
"Is this thing right?" Then at his task
And toil, with purpose strong and true,
'Till done the work God bade him do. .

Various circumstances combined to hinder Dr. Kincaid from returning to Ava, his chosen field, and the one to which he had been specially designated. He was not permitted to pass by the fertile soil of Rangoon and Prome without sowing the seed that soon ripened into harvests of native converts and workers for Jesus. Almost a generation had passed since the first seeds of gospel truth had been sown at Prome by Dr. Judson, and the cruel spirit that had driven him away, had been lost in a desire for knowledge of the Eternal God.

And providence held Dr. Kincaid and the physician designated for the capital until many churches were planted, and the trainer and gleaner stood shoulder to shoulder with the sower over the country from Rangoon and below almost to the capital.

In September, 1855, a messenger from the king waited on Dr. Kincaid to learn when he would visit the Royal City.

Encouraged by an offer from the court, now at Ummerapoora, a few miles up the river from Ava, to send men and boats for the voyage, and furnish the missionary with a house, it was decided.to visit the capital early in 1856, while an opportunity was afforded of meeting the Chinese and Shan caravans to be at the capital in the early spring of that year. This would afford them the opportunity of sending Bibles and tracts into many parts of the dark lands of heathenism, where the name of Jesus had never been heard.

They reached Ummerapoora April 11th, having presented the word by the wayside in numerous villages, to willing hearers.

Ummerapoora then contained a population of three hundred thousand souls. It was noted for its broad, clean and beautiful streets, and was justly regarded as one of the finest cities of the Burman empire.

17

To the north of the city was a beautiful lake, and inviting groves of cocoanut, tamarind, mango and other trees that vied with each other in their efforts to lend beauty to the scene.

Among the first things done after landing was to send Ko En and Moung-paw-te, his two native helpers, in search of members of the little church formerly at Ava.

The first day they found Ko Shway-nee, whose joy was inexpressible on learning of the arrival of his old teacher and that they might look on each other's faces again.   Dr. Kincaid was equally joyous to know that through all the trials, sufferings and reproaches of seventeen years faith had not left him utterly, though alone and exposed to many a bitter blast of persecution.   Despite the scorn and contempt of the world he had fought the good fight and kept the faith.   Tears of joy rolled down their furrowed cheeks as they met after so many eventful years.

He had the good news for his former teacher that his wife's brother had accepted Christ and desired to accompany them to Prome and receive the rite of baptism.

Jesuit priests and some of the officials attempted

to awaken prejudice against the missionaries in the mind of the king.

But they were unsuccessful and the missionaries were received at the palace with marks of distinction.

Mr. Dawson, the physician, says: "To describe the magnificent establishment would require too much time and space; suffice it to say, it was built mainly of teak wood, laquered, carved and gilded so as to give it an exceedingly imposing appearance." Over the throne was a gorgeous and attractive spire, probably two hundred feet high. "Next to the main building was the treasury, containing the crown jewels; back of this was the garden. On one side the royal tower stood, and at its base stood the palace of the "white elephant." Within the same enclosure was the king's court. Here sat the Woon-gees, or ministers of state, administering laws that affected the whole kingdom. The missionaries interviewed two At-woon-wees, or privy councillors, to whose private office they were led by the collector of government customs. They were kindly received, and asked the nature of their business with the king.

Dr. Kincaid told them he had lived in Ava dur-

ing the reign of Noung-dau-pra, and had left the
capital soon after the ascension to the throne of
Thur-ra-wa-di. "We now come to pay our respects
to his majesty," and to learn whether we may abide
near the 'golden feet.'

Other inquiries followed, as to the profession of
medicine, the diseases subject to the physician's
skill; and, being pleased, they went to see if the
king was at leisure. They remained for a little
while, and were then called by the collector of
customs, and told that the king was not engaged.

Leaving their shoes at the foot of the stairway,
they walked up, and were at once in the presence
of his royal highness, the king of Burma. His
age was forty-one; his height five feet and seven
inches. He had a well-developed head and noble
brow, of pleasing countenance, thoughtful mind,
and cheerful temper, with benevolent heart. He
was well but not lavishly dressed. Both his features
and complexion were of the ordinary Burman type.

"Seating ourselves," says Dr. Kincaid, "on the
mats, as did everybody except his majesty, and
throwing our feet back into a most awkward and
painful posture, with our hands upraised, we made

our bow in the usual fashion observed at this court. The king nodded his recognition.

About thirty persons were present, who sat in a semi-circle, and four sword-bearers, with their swords before them.

"The monarch was seated on a crimson velvet carpet, fringed with silk, and spread out on an elevated floor of the adjoining but open apartment." A bolster reposed against one of the gilded posts of the room, against which the king reclined, as he saw fit.

They were formally introduced as American sayahs (teachers) by the privy councillors.

The king at once inquired the object of the missionaries in coming to the capital. With some caution and solicitude about the results that might follow, they informed the king that one object was to present their respects to his majesty, and another was to procure from him the privilege of making the capital the home of themselves and their families. The king then wanted to know what the missionaries proposed to do, and learned it was the purpose of Drs. Kincaid and Dawson to open a school for children and medical dispensary for the sick and suffering.

The king now inquired the distance between
Burma and America, and the time required by sail
vessels or steamers to make the trip from one to
the other, and after much inquiry about the government in America—her relations to France, to
England, and the results of the two wars between
England and the United States, he asked: "Have
you a king in America?" When informed that the
United States government was a republic, in which
all the officers were chosen by the people, the president or chief magistrate being elected every four
years, he shook his head and said it was an unwise
arrangement.   And after some further inquiry as
to whether locating at his capital would affect their
relations with their own government, he again
inquired the object of their visit to Ummerapoora,
"intimating somewhat pleasantly that merchants
wished to acquire property and riches, scientific
travelers passed through to observe the formation
and curiosities of the country, while the object of
others was not quite so clear or creditable.

"This was the hardest remark made," and the
missionaries were quick to give credit for it to the
wily Jesuit, and repeated their purpose to start a
school and dispensary.   When the king interposed,

"Burman children do not want to study English," the reply of Dr. Kincaid was: "We do not purpose teaching the Burman children the English language," but observed that they ought to be taught knowledge.

His majesty now wanted to know when they could come, and began to inquire about commerce, and expressed his desire to encourage trade as much as possible.

He requested the missionaries to write to the newspapers of America of his purpose to promote trade, and wished American merchants to settle in his empire, and improve the opportunities of growing rich.

He was grand nephew to Mekara prince, the most celebrated scholar and learned man in the Burman empire.

After a two hours' conference the king arose, and throwing his arms across his breast, and looking toward Drs. Kincaid and Dawson said: "If you have feelings of regard for me—in short, if you love me, *come soon*, *come soon*, and I will pay all your expenses." He then retired to his private chamber, and sent a lad for the books just presented him by the missionaries.

After a short stay at the capital, the missionaries returned to Prome and Rangoon, with the king's permission to abide at the capital, and greatly encouraged with the outlook for establishing a mission in the capital as soon as others could come from America to occupy the fields they must leave to take up the work at the capital.

In January, 1856, another visit was made to the Royal City by the missionaries and their families, who were most kindly received, and urged to take up their abode in the Royal City. They found the king's brother anxious to commit to the care of Dr. Kincaid ten or a dozen young men selected from the first families, to be taken to America for education in the higher branches of mechanical science, but it was decided best to substitute a literary course at the "Dareton College," Calcutta.

"While such thoughts engaged his royal highness, the king's mind was occupied with the project of an embassy to the United States. To this service Dr. Kincaid was chosen, and, after some hesitation, accepted the appointment of the king, and hastened to prepare for a speedy trip to the home of his youth.

CHAPTER XXIV.

SERVING THE KING.

I rose up and did the King's business.—Dan. viii. 27.

Accepting the appointment of the king of Burma, Dr. Kincaid was given charge of the royal letter that should make known to the government of the United States at Washington, the wishes of the king.

This appointment was more willingly accepted because Mrs. Kincaid's health demanded a change of climate. But for this fact, Dr. Kincaid would scarcely have left his mission work for a day to go on business for an earthly king.

No time was lost in preparing and starting on the journey, that seemed to give hope of a recovery of Mrs. Kincaid's health.

Shortly after his arrival in America, he proceeded to Washington, and, without delay, delivered the royal letter, sealed with the king's seal, and inclosed in a elegant ivory box, lined with crimson velvet.

The following is the literal translation of the royal letter:

"His majesty, whose glory is like the rising sun, ruling over the kingdoms of Tho-na-pa-yon-te, Yon-pa-de-pa, and all the eastern principalities, whose chiefs walk under golden umbrellas, lord of Sadden, the king of elephants, and lord of many white elephants, whose descent is from the royal race of Alompra; also the great lords and officers of state, ever bowing before his majesty as water lilies around the throne, to direct and superintend the affairs of the empire, send salutations to the President and great officers of State residing in the City of Washington, and ruling over many great countries in the continent of America.

His majesty, whose shadow, like that of the royal race, falls over the entire kingdom, desires to govern so as to promote wise and useful regulations, such as the greatest of rulers has ever made it his study to accomplish.

His majesty is aware that it has always been the custom of great rulers to be on terms of friendship with other nations, and to pursue measures tending to perpetuate amity.

As the American teacher, Rev. E. Kincaid, has

come to the royal city, without hindrance, and he
has permission to come to the royal city without
hindrance, and he has permission to go in and out
of the royal palace when he pleases, and has permission to look on the royal countenance, he will
be able to address the President of the United
States on *all subjects* pertaining to the government
and kingdom of Burma. Should this royal kingdom and the great country of America form a
friendly intercourse, there is on our part a desire
that the two great countries, through all coming
generations, may cultivate friendly relations, and
that the merchants and common people, and all
classes, may be greatly benefited. For this purpose
this royal letter is committed to Dr. Kincaid.

Should he be charged with a letter from the
President and great officers of state, to bring to the
royal city of Ava, for his majesty and the court,
and should the President and great officers say, Let
the two countries be on terms of friendship, and
that our children and grandchildren, and all merchants and the common people, may, through all
generations, reap great advantage—should such
a message come, it will be heard with great
pleasure."

The duties of Dr. Kincaid as ambassador were soon and easily accomplished, and when he had accomplished a much more difficult task, of which we will speak further on, he received from the President the following reply to the royal letter brought from the king of Burma :

James Buchanan, President of the United States, of America,

To His Majesty, the King of Ava, whose glory is like the rising sun, ruling over the kingdoms of Thu-na-pa-yonte, Ton-pa-de-pa, and all the Eastern principalities, whose chiefs walk under golden umbrellas; Lord of Sadden, the King of Elephants, and Lord of many White Elephants, whose descent is from the royal race of Alompra; Greeting:

"I have received from the Rev. Eugenio Kincaid the letter which he informs me your majesty delivered to him in April, 1856, of the Christian era. It has been a gratification to me to learn from that communication that so worthy a citizen of the United States as Dr. Kincaid has had free access to your majesty. It would be a further gratification if others of my countrymen who might resort to your majesty's dominions as merchants or as travelers might also be hospitably received. Your majesty may be assured that the subjects of Burma who may visit this country shall be received in the same manner.

We heartily reciprocate your majesty's wish for the cultivation of friendly relations between the two countries, and as we have no interest, the promotion of which, so far as can be foreseen, would render it necessary to desire that your majesty's sovereignty should be diminished, or in any way put in jeopardy, we trust that peace and good will may be perpetual between us.

This letter will be delivered to you by Dr. Kincaid, whom I have authorized to make known to your majesty orally, also, the amicable sentiments of the government and people of the United States towards your majesty and your majesty's subjects.

And so I pray the Almighty to have your majesty in His safe and holy keeping.

Written at Washington this 19th day of May, Anno Domini, 1857.

JAMES BUCHANAN,

By the President.

LEWIS CASS, Secretary of State.

The more difficult undertaking of Dr. Kincaid on this visit was the adjustment of difficulties existing between the executive committee at Boston and a large number of the missionaries.

"These difficulties had now become so involved as to require a full and clear statement of all the facts, in order that the integrity and honor of brethren in the foreign field might be vindicated. As one of their number, bound to each by strong fraternal ties, and familiar with all the points involved in the several cases, Dr. Kincaid came forward and stood nobly for their defense.

"In his earnest vindication, as published in *The American Baptist* and *Christian Chronicle*, may be found the principles for which Dr. Kincaid contended, as well as the motives which prompted him to take so conspicuous a part in this perplexing controversy."

"The views set forth in his vindication were not reached in haste, nor advanced in a retaliative spirit of controversy," but from a sense of duty to both parties, and for the good of the Master in bringing about a better understanding.

"From the beginning of his missionary life he had boldly contended, with all his prominent associates, that the relationship existing between God's ambassadors who are sent to the foreign field and the religious organization through which they derive their support, is not that of *principal* and

agent, employers and *employed*, but strictly one of
'*brotherly equality*,' a relationship requiring them
to look upon each other as *fellow laborers* in the
gospel.

Hence, when the claim was officially put forth
that "*The authority of the· Board is absolute*,"
and when that authority, through the executive
committee, issued instructions demanding "*acqui-
escence*," under the claim of an 'absolute' power,
a power never conceded by the missionaries, and
which they could not comply with, except at the
costly sacrifice of their individual responsibility,
Dr. Kincaid felt himself bound to protest against
such usurped authority, claiming for himself and
for his brethren the right of '*reciprocal direction*,'
and contending that no change should be made
by either party without '*the consent of the other*.'

In advocating this principle, Dr. Kincaid was
led to speak of particular instances in which he
believed it had been openly violated. He referred
particularly to the case of Mr. Vinton, who was
regarded as refractory, in having without authority removed from Maulmain to Rangoon. Dr. Kincaid, after fully explaining the circumstances that
led to that important change, concludes by saying,

"Did Mr. Vinton go to Rangoon on his own responsibility? One thousand Karen Christians called him to 'come over and help them.' Humanity with imploring voice called him; above all, the Providence of God, in clear and distinct language, called him to the work. Dare he sit still, and say to these suffering Karens, and to weeping humanity, and above all, to the Providence of God, "Let me first go and obtain permission from those who claim dictatorial power over me." Dare he so insult the Providence of God, and mock the entreaties of God's suffering people? Should he say, 'I am a *hireling*,' and look not after the torn and scattered flock? Did Mr. Vinton go to Rangoon, on his own responsibility? Shame, shame on such gross and fabulous statements.

Never, since the day Paul was called into Macedonia, has there been a clearer case of duty to go in the name of Christ. Had it been my case, under similar circumstances, no opposition on the part of man would have been regarded as of the slightest moment. I should have brushed them as cobwebs from my path. What power is that which thrusts itself between the ambassador of Christ in a heathen land, and the God of missions? What power is that which claims to keep the consciences of men who are planting churches on heathen shores?

To the exercise of this power, claiming the right to give direction, but resisted by several devoted and successful missionaries, Dr. Kincaid ascribed all the difficulty which had for years hindered missionary operations.

It was this, he said, that had subjected them to the grave charge of "disregarding regulations," and "setting at naught instructions;" and, impressed with the danger and evil consequent upon such an assumption of power, he said: The cry of 'insubordination,' 'disregard of regulations,' 'setting at naught instructions,' was the cry of desperation. Oppression caused a revolt, not against regulations, but against outrage and wrong. "Regulations were never *knowingly* disregarded. Oppression arouses, in self-defense, all but slaves." Then, he added, 'Let any man or set of men be armed with dictatorial power, and there may be the exhibition of a *strong government*, to carry any measure, however unwise; to silence every murmur, however reasonable; and to crush all opposition, however just, as Louis Napoleon put France under his feet.

18

Let every subject of importance be thoroughly ventilated and sifted. Let discussion, untrammeled by threats, be invited. Let all the aids of testimony, and the lights of experience and history, be invoked. Let opinion grapple with opinion. This will be the most precious guaranty for the avoidance of evil, the security of sacred rights, and the preservation of truth. If infallibility is ascribed to one set of men, in such a sense as to require all their official acts to be sanctioned without examination, then a principle has been adopted abhorrent to protestant Christianity.''

''The fearless avowal of sentiments like these had the effect to awaken, in some quarters, no little opposition, and not a few were disposed to regard their utterance a crime worthy to be treated as ecclesiastical treason.''

But neither fear nor favor influenced him for a moment, to withhold the declaration of his honest convictions; and, with the same manliness which marked his whole life, he hesitated not to speak what he believed to be the truth, and shunned not the responsibility assumed in resisting what he felt to be an encroachment on the Christian liberty of himself and his missionary brethren.

As on his two former visits to America, Dr. Kincaid's earnest addresses were everywhere heard with the deepest interest, and his moving appeals in behalf of the perishing heathen never failed to meet with a cheerful and liberal response.

But, in addition to the service rendered to the general cause of missions, he was successful, through the voluntary contributions made at the close of his last public efforts in Philadelphia and New York, in raising a fund of about a thousand dollars, which was judiciously expended in the purchase of a large assortment of educational works, and also of a number of astronomical instruments for use in the Karen schools at Rangoon.

CHAPTER XXV.

Dr. Kincaid, leaving his family behind at New York, embarked for Glasgow, arriving there after a pleasant voyage of fifteen days. Visited and preached for a few weeks in Scotland and England, then taking the overland or mail route to Calcutta, he landed December 5th, after a pleasant and most interesting voyage; and early in January, 1858, located in Prome, where he was joined in due time by his family, and began those missionary labors that employed him during his last stay in Burma. His time was spent mainly at Prome and in the country adjacent, and going from village to village and town to town, strengthening the brethren and encouraging them to reach out and extend their efforts to the regions beyond.

Among the facts connected with his closing years of mission work at Prome, one who was on the field during this period furnishes the following:

"I know that after he went to Prome, his time

was spent in traveling from town to town, preaching to Burmans, Karens, Shyens, Shans. Wherever
he could find an audience, whether of one or one
hundred, he gave them the gospel. When he
found a people whose language he did not understand, he was not deterred one moment; he got
an interpreter and preached Christ to them. He
had none of the narrow-mindedness that charac-
terizes so many men, and makes them unable to
see more than the one people to whom they may
have been designated. To him the field was the
world; and he was sent to garner souls, no matter
of what name, or race, or language"—whether at
home or abroad. He was just as glad to meet a
caravan of traders coming to the serpentine amber
mines to trade, and give them the gospel, as to
preach to his people in the church at home.

"As a preacher his power was something wonderful," says one who often heard him in the field.
"I doubt if ever Burma has seen a greater. Indeed,
I regard him as one of the greatest men that the
missionary union ever sent out." "Others have
had more said of them and their work, but no one
ever did more true and lasting service for the cause
of missions."

Another, who witnessed some of his devotions and toils on the field, says of him: "He toiled while others took their ease; his excursions into the regions beyond were not infrequent. These excursions were often matters of great self-denial and hardship, as much of the time he was compelled to lie on the ground without bed or pillow. Oftentimes his saddle served the purpose of pillow, while the blanket that went under the saddle would cover a portion of the ground on which he lay. He was a fine horseman, and very much enjoyed a good ride, and never feared it would injure his spirituality to ride faster than a jog of a trot. He cared well for his horse; fed well, and rode likewise.

"No one would entertain a company at table better than he, and while talking he forgot all about eating." "One day on the English ship *Tudor*, on a voyage from Cape Town to Calcutta, in 1850, some of the officers made a bet that they would cheat Dr. Kincaid out of his dinner and he would not know it. As soon as grace was said, some one started him on some of his experiences among the Dakoits (robbers). The servants had orders to remove his plate at the end of every course, whether he had finished or not. The soup went away untouched, and so did the fish, and so on through a long dinner of some eight or ten courses, .and by a judicious word thrown in now and then, when he showed signs of attacking what was on his plate, they contrived to get to the coffee without his having tasted a mouthful. As he drained the little cup of coffee, some one said: 'Mr. Kincaid, I'm afraid you haven't had much dinner.' 'O, yes,' he exclaimed, 'I have eaten plentifully,' and he thought he had.''

In 1865, broken down in health, he took final leave of the scenes of his missionary life, of his brothers and sisters in church relations, won from heathenism by the power of the word preached, and leave of the school where his companion had been daily engaged in teaching the Burmese females.

They embarked on board the *Verona*, a sailing vessel, enjoyed a pleasant voyage, visited in England and Scotland, and reached America March 17th, 1866. The family visited a brother Thomas in New York city for a time, where Dr. Kincaid had quite a serious illness, and when sufficiently recovered to do so, was advised to go to the mountains, that with care he might possibly live a year. He located at Norristown, Penn., and during his stay of nearly three years in that place, he traveled through many of the states kindling missionary zeal, and endeavoring to enlist the churches more generally in missionary enterprises. About the end of the third year, Dr. Kincaid removed his family from Norristown to 1735 Park Avenue, Philadelphia.

In 1869 Dr. Cowie, Sanitary Commissioner General of British India, then on a visit to Dr. Kincaid, his father-in-law, advised a trip to Kansas, which was made and gave such encouragement to Dr. Kincaid by its pure, refreshing breezes and broad, inviting and beautiful prairies, that it was decided that he should pass his last days in this most delightful country.

But one of the saddest occasions of life was to be met before this plan should be carried into execution, namely: the death of their daughter Mary—Mrs. J. S. Ingraham. This occurred in 1871. The same year Dr. Kincaid and family located just a few miles west of Girard on a nice elevation where the pure, refreshing breezes added, no doubt, many years of pleasure to a most eventful and worthy life.

They at once identified themselves with Girard Baptist Church, and always showed a deep interest in its welfare and ready hands to help in all its work.

When I began preaching for this church in the autumn of 1877, the membership numbered about thirty, with a debt on the building that gave us considerable anxiety. Once while making an effort to raise this money Dr. Kincaid said, "I have two cows and am willing to sell one of them that this debt shall be paid."

And I am persuaded if his many friends east and west could have beheld his earnestness of manner, and heard with what tender solicitude he talked of a Sabbath home for the little church, struggling under difficulties for existence, most cheerfully and heartily would they respond to the call for help to perpetuate his memory through the ages to come in the erection of a suitable and much-needed "memorial church edifice."

I preached for nearly four years at a school house nearer Dr. Kincaid's residence than the church in Girard. One thing I never can forget in connection with this work, and that is the faithfulness of this aged veteran in his attendance on divine worship. Often his team was the first on the ground. I remember one bitter cold morning I drove six miles to this school house and found Dr. Kincaid and his daughters Genie and Helen, standing outside the school house door shivering with cold, waiting for the "volunteer" sexton to open the door and fire up. I could always count on Dr. Kincaid being present when able to sit in his carriage and drive, though unable to feed himself.

I frequently visited the family as pastor, and quite often conveyed parties from Girard to his place that would come by rail to see and converse with him who had "endured" such "hardships as a good soldier of Jesus Christ."

He possessed an almost unlimited fund of knowledge, was a good conversationalist, and seemed never to tire of entertaining and instructing the many guests who entered his home. "He was fond of telling how he shocked Dr. and Mrs. Wade once, and undid the effect of some good advice they had just given.

They were in the habit of taking the new missionaries in and explaining to them how dangerous

it was to eat freely of the fruit of the country.
They were exceedingly cautious, and were particularly afraid of pineapple. One thin slice was, in
their estimation, all that could be eaten in safety
at once, and that only by a person of good diges-
tion. In a letter to Mrs. Moore, Mrs. Luther says:
"Your father was at the tiffin table (a lunch
between breakfast and dinner) one day with quite
a little party of new missionaries, and Mr. Wade
had been cautioning them about too free indul-
gence in fruit. 'Yes,' your father chimed.
'*Moderation.*' Now, about pineapples, one must
be careful—be moderate, as Brother Wade says.
Now, I should think one or two pineapples at a
time is all anyone ought to eat.' I can see him
now throw his head back and laugh at the horror
that his words caused. When cholera was
especially prevailing he would say: 'One must be
careful about food. Cucumbers I find to be the
best thing to keep off cholera. Yes, eat freely of
cucumbers and you will be all right.' He was very
active, a hearty eater, and seldom experienced any
uneasiness or distress from anything he might eat.

CHAPTER XXVI.

HIS KANSAS HOME.

It would afford me great pleasure to have the reader and the many friends of Dr. Kincaid and his family take a stroll with me over the Kansas farm, and through the fruit and flower gardens where the last days of his earthly life were spent.

He had built for them a comfortable house, on a beautiful elevation overlooking the country for miles in every direction.

This house was surrounded with fruits and groves of forest trees, planted and cultivated with care. The house stood several yards from the road that run by the south side of the farm. Nicely kept driveways angled through beds of flowering shrubs and plants, some of which were brought from the mission fields where he had labored, some from other parts of the world.

Mrs. Kincaid, though quite infirm, took great comfort in caring for these flowers, and making a most cheerful, happy home for their declining days.

This home was sold, and one purchased in Girard, and the very day set for removal from the old homestead the Master said, "It is enough, come up higher," and the church privileges Dr. Kincaid so much desired to enjoy were exchanged for the scenes in glory long awaiting him. His companion only lingered with us three weeks longer until she went to join him whose toils and labors she had shared for so many years, full of work for Jesus.

I had read the "Hero Missionary" when a young man, and if I ever had an ardent desire for anything it was to be a missionary; but now I can see plainly the wisdom of God in not opening the way for the fulfillment of that ardent desire. And, if on this effort divine approval may rest I shall feel satisfied.

I fully appreciate the feelings of a most devoted friend of Dr. Kincaid, who says:

"I am glad and yet sorry, to hear that his life is to be written. I feel that *no* pen can do him justice. In my love and admiration for his wonderful character, I am jealous lest it should not have the masterly portrayal that it deserves."

Not a page has been written without a consciousness of my inability to give a portrayal of the *love* and *power* of his life.   Nor could I feel it best to be wholly silent, because I may not do in a masterly way what I feel must be done.   So if some little good may be accomplished by the imperfect portrayal his life gets here, maybe some one will be induced to look through his life to the perfect pattern of which his was only designed to be in some parts a copy.

"No memoir of him will ever tell half the story; but up yonder is the record."

When I stood by his reclining chair, where night after night, he was propped up, because his asthma was so bad he could not lie down, and he was liable to go at any moment into the spirit world, I scarce could keep from envying him the journey he was so soon to take; but when I remembered my reward would not be according to his toil, I was willing to linger and labor on so as to make my coming into heaven more like his should be.

It has been thought no larger number of Karens would welcome to the better shore any toiler for Jesus than would welcome him whose life and labors have been sketched here.

Sister Luther says, "Some day when some of us get there with the few souls we have garnered here below, and we see one go by with shining garments, stately mein and a crown that is ablaze with stars that shimmer and sparkle like the sun for their exceeding number and we ask wonderingly, Who is that? The angels shall make answer, That is Eugenio Kincaid.''

Gathered about him will not be a mere handful from one province or empire but multitudes will gather about him as the instrumental cause of their salvation, and prove the affinity of soul between him and them, as expressed by him, while nearing the turbid waters of death, when he said, '' Brother Webb, if I were wholly dependent, I would want to be among the native Christians of Burma. I know they would not see me lack.''

He did not lack in his comfortable home here but only expressed his confidence in a people whom he had seen won from heathenism and idol worship to salvation and the true and living God.

He retained his mental faculties to the very last and although so palsied that he had not been able to feed himself for years before his death, his courage and daring never failed him.

On a February evening before his death in April, and when past eighty-six years of age, he and his daughter Genie were at Girard in a single buggy. On the shortest way home there was no bridge over Lightning Creek, a stream at that season of the year generally waist deep and perhaps four rods in width.

. The stream was frozen over, he thought sufficiently solid to allow them to drive over on the ice with safety. Genie dissented and wanted to go a mile south to a good iron bridge. He said, "We have not time and shall have no difficulty in crossing; go ahead." They had gone only far enough from the shore to make retreat impossible, when the buggy cut through the ice, which also gave way under the horse in such manner as to get both parties into the water waist deep but they finally reached the other shore in safety, of one mind about the bearing qualities of the ice, wet and wiser. The distance of three miles between them and home was soon passed, Genie complaining somewhat. But I well remember how George related to me this occurrence the second day afterward. He said, "Father don't seem to mind a thing like that. It would kill me, but father regards such happenings as mere trifles," and so it seemed, for he experienced not the slightest inconvenience from it after exchanging his wet suit for a dry one.

Dr. Kincaid was not a man of such prepossessing and overmastering appearance as to awe men into subjection, or the adoption of his plans. He was not a born organizer or commander, but an incessant worker—tender and loving, yet firm as granite. In his death our denomination and the Christian world at large lost a man of devotion, zeal and power, whose life is inscribed on the pages of history, and one who has been largely instrumental in moulding and shaping the character and destiny of multitudes in different nations of the earth.

His missionary labors in Western New York and through Pennsylvania, bound the people to him, and drew their prayers and funds to the support of missions, both home and foreign, and to the founding and endowment of Lewisburg University.

The sum of his influence for good and for God —at home and abroad—can never be measured this side of eternity. His sterling integrity and unswerving devotion to truth and right, and his fear of nothing but to do wrong were traits of character so peculiarly prominent in his make-up, that

I deem it wise and good, in this age of "fiction" and "novel" reading, to portray in some sense a life stranger than fiction, possessed of a love for Jesus and lost men stronger than death—a courage that could meet the robbers of Northern Burma, the king's court at Ava, the governor at Rangoon, or the council at Maulmain, and swerve not a moment from the right in any of these surroundings.

Grand old "Hero" of many a hard fight,
Always found on the side of truth and right,
Until God spoke out, "My servant, 'well done,'
Inherit an heirship with Jesus, my son."

THE "PHILADELPHIA CONFERENCE OF BAPTIST MINISTERS."

1420 CHESTNUT STREET,
PHILADELPHIA, PA., April 23, 1883.

At a regular meeting of the Conference held this A. M. the following MINUTE, *as prepared by Rev'd G. M. Spratt, D. D., was read and unanimously adopted:—*

"WHEREAS, *a well-ordered Christian life, full of deep interest in the history of Missions, especially in connection with the "American Baptist Missionary Union," as well as a life closely identified with the foundation and continued prosperity of the "University at Lewisburg," and other services rendered to the Denomination as a Missionary for several years in the central portion of our State, terminated on the 3d instant, in the death of*

EUGENIO KINCAID, D. D.,

therefore,

Resolved, That we deem it fitting to place on record, as a Conference, our high appreciation of his valuable services during more than half a century.

Resolved, That we express to the family of our deceased brother, our warm sympathy, in their bereavement, and forward them a copy of the above MINUTE."

ATTEST:

Rev. Eugenio Kincaid, D. D., was buried in the beautiful city cemetery at Girard, Kansas, April 5th, 1883, and Mrs. Barbara McBain Kincaid was buried at his side April 29th of the same year.

Peacefully may they "rest from their labors while their works do follow them," until the Master calls the sleeping dust to join the disembodied spirits gone on before.

His mansion complete in the better land,
Arranged and built by the Master's hand,
Was stored with the precious sheaves of grain
His toil had gleaned from the wasting plain.

Not a vacant room or a barren wall,
But garnered full, each room and hall,
Of the trophies won from the open field,
Whom the Holy Spirit for Christ had sealed.

And when he stood on the golden shore,
Beside his mansion, of choicest store;
With joy he heard from his gracious Lord,
"As thy toil was great, so thy reward."

And Jesus put on his brow a crown,
With a star for every soul laid down,
Then gave him the mansion he'd stored so well
As his own, in which forever to dwell.

THE END.

www.ingramcontent.com/pod-product-compliance
Lightning Source LLC
Chambersburg PA
CBHW030621030726
47497CB00006B/1589